A Dungeon's Soul

Book 3 of Adventures on Brad

by

Tao Wong

Copyright

This is a work of fiction. Names, characters, businesses, places, events and incidents are either the products of the author's imagination or used in a fictitious manner. Any resemblance to actual persons, living or dead, or actual events is purely coincidental.

This book is licensed for your personal enjoyment only. This book may not be re-sold or given away to other people. If you would like to share this book with another person, please purchase an additional copy for each recipient. If you're reading this book and did not purchase it, or it was not purchased for your use only, then please return to your favorite book retailer and purchase your own copy. Thank you for respecting the hard work of this author.

Books in the
Adventures on Brad series

A Healer's Gift
An Adventurer's Heart
A Dungeon's Soul
The Arena's Call
The Adventurer's Bond
The Forest's Silence

Contents

Chapter 1

Dawn light filtered through the wooden shutters of Daniel Chai's room in the Spinning Top. He shivered, pulling his blankets closer to his body for a moment as the late autumn morning chill made itself known to him. Long years of discipline forced him to sit up now that he was awake. He ran a hand through his hair, smiling slightly at the uneven cut that Khy'ra, his girlfriend, had given him. She was a dangerous Adventurer, a beautiful Elf, and a kindly Healer, but the one thing she was not was a decent barber.

After stretching slowly to his full five foot eight inches, Daniel walked to the windows after wiping himself down, sliding a shirt back on. He threw the shutters open and looked out at the sprawling city of wood and stone before him, then leaned outwards slightly as he stared at the center of town to spot the Dungeon entrance and the Adventurers' Guild. Early as it was, he could see streams of Adventurers entering and exiting the Dungeon, traversing the pathway between Guild and Dungeon to sell their loot before resting.

The Karlak Dungeon had reopened in the last few days after being closed for weeks as the Dungeon reconfigured itself. The wave of relief that had risen through the city when it was made clear that it was still a Beginner Dungeon had been palatable. As every Adventurer had to start again from the first Level, the Adventurers' Guild had instituted a lottery system to stagger entry. Eventually, the more experienced Adventurers would trickle down to the lower levels and entry would no longer need to be staggered, as the Adventurers would all be spread out across its many levels. Eventually.

Daniel sighed again, pulled his head back in, and finished dressing. Unfortunately, their party had drawn a slot for tomorrow, leaving them to wait another day. Weeks without their most important income source meant that he needed to work whatever jobs he could find on the quest board if he wanted to eat tomorrow. Staying in bed was not an option.

Walking down the stairs, he waved to Elise, the Spinning Top's owner, who was delivering food to the floor. The matronly blonde smiled at Daniel, nodding to a free table while she delivered watered-down beer, wine, and a mix of eggs, bacon, and leafy greens to the table. Daniel idly noted that the plates were nearly overflowing with greens as the very last harvest had been pulled from the ground. Soon, only canned vegetables and a small variety of magically preserved vegetables would be available.

"Morning, Elise," Daniel greeted the innkeeper as she arrived with his breakfast. Elise just flashed him a smile, too busy to chat while he dug into the meal with gusto. As he finished up, Elise dropped off a pair of wrapped lunches at his table.

Outside, having retrieved his leather armor, shield, and mace, Daniel quickly joined the flow of humanity as he headed to the Guild. Daniel casually eyed the crowds who were mostly made up of human townsfolk with the occasional glimpse of a Beastkin. Early as it was, most Adventurers were either already in the Dungeon or still asleep. Once he arrived at the Adventurers' Guild, he found his partner, Asin, waiting for him.

"Morning, Asin," he greeted his friend and fellow party member. The smaller Catkin was crouched on the stairs that led up to the building, licking at her paw while her tail lazily waved in the air behind her. Jade eyes glinted in amusement as Daniel handed her the packet of food, which she quickly slipped into her bag, ensuring it was strapped in and out of the way of her additional throwing knives.

"Daniel," Asin purred. The Catkin as always kept her speaking to the minimum, being one of the unlucky few who found it painful to speak in the human tongue of Brad. Unfortunately, as hard as Daniel worked at it, he found it difficult to shape his throat and tongue to speak the common Beastkin language.

"Checked out the quest board yet?" Daniel asked as he walked up the stairs. Asin stood smoothly, her movements all feline grace. At the shake of Asin's head, Daniel nodded contentedly. Inside, the Adventurers' Guild buzzed as Adventuring parties cashed out Mana Stones, hung out regaling each other with tales of the new floors, and generally made a mess. Asin's ears perked up as she swiveled her head from side to side, listening in on the conversation. Being the third day of the Dungeon opening, talk mostly centered around the first floor and as such, Asin learnt nothing new.

The quest board was literally a pair of rolling wooden boards upon which the attendants at the Guild posted new requests. The board itself was separated into three portions depicting the most common quest types—Delivery, Collection, and Miscellaneous. Unlike the previous few weeks, the board was not stripped bare of all quests as more and more Adventurers went back to the Dungeon to earn coin.

Lips pursed, Daniel slowly read through the posted offers. Unlike many of his peers, the former Miner had been taught to read, so he ignored the symbols posted on the bottom right for the illiterate, instead studying the board for a suitable option.

"Ah, brave heroes! The morning's fire greets you all!" The roared greeting makes Asin wince. Everyone in the Guild briefly turned to view the youthful barbarian who was the cause of the ruckus. Standing nearly a foot taller than Daniel, the blond-haired, tunic-clad muscular Northerner towered over the Adventurers within, a friendly smile on his face as he walked in. Carrying only a single, large sword, the barbarian strode over to the quest board, his grin widening as he spotted Asin and Daniel.

"Morning, Omrak," Daniel greeted the youngster, shuffling over slightly to give the barbarian space.

"This? Is this quest worthy of a hero?" A brief few seconds later, Omrak was pointing out a quest with a meaty finger.

"Uhhh …" Daniel read the quest notice, lips twitching. "That's a request for beaters for the upcoming Fall Hunt. It's a few days away and you'd need to make your way there. Not bad pay though."

"Ah …" Omrak rumbled, staring at the quest. Daniel raised an eyebrow and Omrak shrugged as he answered the unspoken question. "I have no party. I must wait a few more days before entering the Dungeon. This quest work, it is less than heroic but better than the docks."

"No luck with finding a party so far?" Daniel asked.

"No. I fear I must wait for a new group or grow strong myself," Omrak said, clapping a hand to his chest.

"Well, we're going in tomorrow …" Daniel began to say before he was elbowed in the side by Asin. She snarled at him, making him blink.

"Hero Asin …?"

"Later," Asin growled as she dragged Daniel to a nearby booth. She lowered her voice then, snarling at him. "No offer."

"But why?" asked Daniel. "It won't be for long and he needs some help."

"First floor. Lousy stones. Split three way," Asin said, her tail lashing out behind her.

"Uhh …" Daniel quickly parsed the sentences together before he blinked. "You don't want to help Omrak because we won't earn enough?"

Asin nodded firmly, making Daniel grimace.

"He's not earning a lot right now. It won't hurt for him to join us and we could use his help at lower levels. He's roughly on the same level as we are so he wouldn't be holding us back," Daniel said quickly, lining up his arguments.

"Expensive," Asin repeated.

"Yeah, but he can carry more than we can."

Asin paused, clearly taken by that thought. Pressing his advantage, Daniel continued, "You know you can't carry much and neither can I. With more help, we could potentially clear the second floor in a single day."

Asin frowned before she finally answered, "Third."

"That's …"

"Third."

"Fine!" Daniel grimaced, knowing that pushing to do three floors in a single run was going to be difficult. However, the Guild had agreed that any party that managed to make it to the third floor would be eligible to enter the Dungeon at any time. Having won her way, Asin stalked back to the big barbarian who had been watching the argument with interest.

"Join. Carry. Go fast," Asin hissed at the big man, holding her fingers up as she spoke. "Equal share."

Omrak grinned, clapping the diminutive Catkin on the shoulder and staggering her. "Thank you, hero! You shall not find fault in our progress. I shall be your shield, your sword, and your back!"

"Loud!" Asin complained to Daniel as she grabbed a quest off the board and stalked off to join the line awaiting an attendant.

"Omrak, quieter, please," Daniel said, grinning slightly at his Catkin friend, who was rubbing her shoulder discretely.

"Of course, hero!" Omrak said in a stage whisper.

"Tomorrow, at the entrance. Dawn."

"I shall be there. But for now, I must meet with the Master of Docks. I shall avail myself to the boats one last day."

"Yeah, you do that. See you, Omrak." Having said his goodbyes, Daniel strode over to his waiting friend, who held the quest notice out for Daniel to read. He winced as he read it over, grumbling. "Really?"

"Good coin."

"I know …" Daniel sighed again and slipped the quest notice into his pouch. Well, he was asking her to help.

***

Hours later, Daniel stifled a slight groan as he hauled the next basket of fish up the steep hill. As Omrak would have said—this was not a hero's work. However, it was decent-paying work for both of them—at least, so long as the fish were swimming. It was the last week of the run and the Fishermen's Guild had finally opened up fishing on the river, ensuring that the nets and fishing traps were running full-bore. Even if Adventurers were not the preferred day laborers, this week any extra pair of hands was gratefully taken.

Daniel just wished that he was not stuck doing the heavy labor. Unfortunately, like most of the hired Adventurers, he had no Skills or background in crafting, so fixing the nets or the traps was out. His only saving grace here was his strength and endurance, and so he found himself trudging up the hill with baskets filled with fish. In the river, Asin—with her natural grace and her superb aim—was having the time of her life with the nets. Even without a Skill related to fishing, she was pulling a significant number of fish out.

As he came back down the hill, Daniel watched Asin tromp out of the freezing water to warm up against the nearby braziers. Enchanted galoshes kept her feet and thighs warm but did nothing for her torso. Daniel had to hide a smile when she finally exited and shook herself hard, sending droplets of cold water cascading from her fur. A choked snort from behind him told Daniel that he was not the only one to find the wet Catkin amusing.

If he had to spend a day outside of the Dungeon, this was not a bad way to do so. Still, as Daniel stretched and looked up into the sky, he could not help but look forward to the next day.

***

"Daniel," Khy'ra greeted him as she entered her house. "I got your message at the Clinic."

"Khy'ra." He bent forwards, planting a quick kiss on her lips before he turned back to frying the fish. One good thing about working the river today—dinner was easily served. "Everything good at the Clinic?"

"The usual." Khy'ra shrugged. "Nothing that needs your Gift, though if you could spare a few minutes later, we have a few patients that could use a Healing."

Daniel nodded, relieved that he would not be required to use his Gift. A small number, maybe one in a thousand, were Gifted with an ability upon birth. The usefulness and strength of the ability varied but what never did was that the use of a Gift had a cost. For Daniel, that cost of using his Gift was the loss of a portion of his memories, his experience, his Skills. However, his Gift also provided him an uncanny understanding of the body which allowed him to learn and progress in the use of more traditional Healing magic.

"After dinner," Daniel said.

"Of course. Worked the river today?" Khy'ra asked as she walked up beside him, breathing in the aroma of the fried fish. She could smell crushed pepper, the pork fat that she had saved, dried thyme, red peppers, and something else. Brows furrowed, the Elf stared at the tantalizing dish.

"Asin's recipe," Daniel answered, prodding the fish once again before taking it out of the frying pan.

"Should I get the milk then?" Khy'ra teased as she walked to set the table.

"I fixed it," Daniel said proudly. Once again, he was grateful that the Catkin was as dedicated to good food as he was—his journeys in the last few months had taught him that this was not the case with most other Adventuring parties. On the other hand, the Beastkin had a tendency to eat intensely spicy foods—something that puzzled Daniel, considering their expanded senses.

"Oh good," Khy'ra said, and Daniel laughed. As much as Khy'ra complained, he could still recall her stuffing her face without complaint the last time Asin was here cooking for them all.

"You're headed into the Dungeon tomorrow?" Khy'ra asked as she finished setting the table, watching as Daniel fished out the bread from the oven. There were many reasons she cared for this young Adventurer, but the way he fed her certainly helped. A touch of sorrow flickered across her face as she recalled that he would be leaving soon. Like most humans, they stepped into and out of her life.

"Yes. Do you recall the Northerner? Omrak?"

"I've seen him around. Big man."

"Uhh …" Daniel paused, noting the admiring tone in her voice before he shook away the flash of jealousy. "Yes. He'll be joining us. At least for a few levels."

"Mmmm … that's good," Khy'ra said around a mouthful of fish.

Daniel blinked, uncertain of whether she was referring to his cooking or Omrak. Seeing his confusion, Khy'ra's eyes crinkled in humor and Daniel realized she had done it on purpose. Seeing him growl playfully at her, the Elf finally relented.

"It's good that you've gotten more help. There are a lot of Dungeons that can't be completed without more members," Khy'ra clarified. Daniel nodded, knowing what she said was true. However, both he and Asin were workaholics, and finding others who were willing to keep up with them would have been difficult. Daniel, however, had a very good feeling about Omrak.

Biting into the fish himself, Daniel turned the conversation to Khy'ra's day, pushing aside thoughts of the Dungeon and Adventuring. They would have more than enough to discuss tomorrow.

Chapter 2

"Morning, Liev," Daniel greeted the red-haired, scrawny Guild attendant. Leaning against the wooden counter, Daniel proffered their chit in exchange for the entrance seal.

"Daniel, Asin. And Omrak?" Liev stared at the blond giant, lines on his face deepening as he raised an eyebrow in inquiry to the pair. After receiving a confirming nod, Liev just shrugged and added Omrak's name to the seal. "Have you been keeping up with the news?"

"Yes, but best to go over it again," Daniel answered for the group. Asin pursed her lips slightly, eager to leave, but said nothing. Behind, Omrak looped his thumbs in his belt, pushing his giant sword that hung by a shoulder sheath down his chest to the side.

"Right, first floor has Kobolds. No change there," Liev said. "Second floor, we've got Elemental Turtles. Slow but tough. You either need to flip them or shatter their shells. As you know, breaking the shells in combat will decrease the chance that they'll drop when the Dungeon dismisses the body and the Guild is buying the shells. We're paying two copper per shell currently. No traps reported.

"No group has managed to make it to the third floor as yet. The first floor is relatively small—about three-quarters the size of the old first floor. The second floor makes up for it, being about thrice the size. It's a mixture of water pools and caves, so you'll need to be careful about walking around. There are no natural lights and the Guild has not installed any thus far, so you'll need to bring your own for the second floor. An extra pair of clothing is also recommended, and rope."

Having finished his rundown, Liev waited patiently for any questions. Seeing none, he finished.

"That's about it for the Dungeon so far. We did get a letter indicating that we should expect at least a few interested Advanced parties soon."

Daniel grunted at the news, not entirely surprised. The bonus for completing a new Dungeon added to the allure of the unknown was bound to draw some more experienced Adventurers. Even so, Asin hissed slightly, while Omrak was either oblivious to the implications or uncaring, having shown no reaction to the news.

"Thanks, Liev. We'll see you tonight?" Daniel asked.

Liev nodded in agreement, watching the trio leave with a slight smile on his face before he turned to the next group.

***

"Do we have everything we need?" Daniel asked the group on the short walk to the Dungeon entrance. Unlike other cities, which made a big showing of the Dungeon, Karlak's entrance was a simple stone building with large double doors flanking it. Daniel's lips twisted wryly at the sight of the doors—he had never seen them closed other than for the reconstruction.

"About time you got in. Been lazing around?" Ken, the chubby middle-aged town guard, called out to Daniel and Asin when they arrived. He gave a cursory glance at the seal they offered, dropping it into the pouch that waited beside him. "Well, I won't keep you. I expect stories and drinks tonight at the Top, though."

Daniel smiled at the noisy guard, offering a quick nod to Curtzman on the opposite side before he led his party inside. Neither of the other Adventurers had offered much more than a nod to the pair of guards—Asin because the guards generally treated her kind with a significant degree of distrust, and Omrak because his run-ins with the Karlak guard had mostly occurred late at night, and ended up with him in the cells waiting to sober up.

Inside, the stone building led immediately to a familiar grey entranceway. As they reached the entrance, both Daniel and Omrak stepped forwards to lead the way. Daniel twitched, staring at the Northerner who was in the process of unsheathing his greatsword.

"I shall lead the way, Hero Daniel. It shall be my honor to be your shield," Omrak declared.

For a moment, Daniel felt a sense of vertigo as he adjusted his thinking. Omrak was right—being both a bigger, stronger, and more skilled melee fighter, Omrak was the better choice to lead the way. Especially as the first couple of floors had been reported as trapless. Daniel looked over the Northerner again, noting that outside a leather groin cup, Omrak still had not managed to save up for a suit of armor. In fact, aside from his greatsword and a knife that was so big it could be considered a short sword itself, the barbarian was the most lightly equipped of the group.

Daniel, was dressed in the breastplate and pauldrons of his old leather armor. While he would have preferred to use his newly acquired suit of iron armor, the dangers of the watery second level kept him dressed minimally. If he did fall in, he could discard his shield and mace and swim to the surface with what he currently wore.

Asin, was equipped with a light surcoat of untreated leather, a pair of crossed bandoleers holding throwing knives across her chest, and more strapped to her legs. On her hips, she carried a pair of larger fighting knives that she used when she needed to get close. Hanging from a series of straps behind her, were the bolos she had purchased in Peel. To top it all, he spotted the enchanted lightning bracers and the enchanted Shield gorget that she wore instead of more powerful armor.

All three Adventurers of course carried their other gear, packs filled with rope, lamps, food packets, trap balls, and other essential delving gear. Asin, catching his serious study of their equipment, snorted lightly and Daniel gave a wry smile. Okay, it was only the first few floors of a Beginner Dungeon.

***

The first floor was a total sense of déjà vu for the entire group. The low ceilings and narrow passageways meant that Omrak spent a significant portion of the time bent over, carrying his sword in one hand. The smooth, Mana-imbued stones that made up the passageways, glowed with a soft blue light that offered the group enough illumination to see easily, though they all knew that after a few hours they would feel the subtle strain.

What was different was the sheer number of Adventurers. Early as they were, staggered entry or not, the number of Adventurers walking through the first floor was unusual. It was no busy city street, but for a Dungeon, it could be considered uncomfortably busy. Many of the Adventurers held maps in their hands, sketching in new corridors and marking intersections, while others rushed down the passages as they attempted to either locate more monsters to kill or complete mapping the floor for the experience bonus.

In either case, after a long hour of not locating a single monster, both Asin and Omrak were growing impatient.

"Bad luck," Asin grumbled, jerking her head to the Northerner.

"Asin …" Daniel began. It was not as if the crowding was Omrak's fault.

"My blade hungers for blood too, Hero Asin," Omrak said. "Though perhaps we can seek blood in less cramped quarters."

The loud reverberations of Omrak's declaration made Asin wince, her sensitive ears twitching. She growled softly, about to chastise him again, when she heard something. Having glanced back to look at his friend, Daniel saw her ears twitch and her tail straighten.

"What is it?" Daniel asked softly.

"Kobold," she answered, and pointed down the hallway. The word had not fully left her mouth before Omrak let out a yell of excitement, charging the monster. As he took the corner, he barreled into the wiry, long-limbed Kobold who was rushing to check out the noise as well.

Bowled over, the short monster was only beginning to struggle to his feet before a massive fist, swung in a tight, left hook, connected with its face. It lifted the Kobold entirely off its feet and slammed the top of its head into the wall, cracking it open. It was not a fact that Omrak noticed as his foot swung forwards to end the fight.

Slain, the Kobold's brownish-gray body glittered and broke apart, the corruption by Ba'al dispersed. In return, the Kobold left an unused, rusty shiv and a tiny Mana Stone. The Mana Stone was the core of the monster, the way that Erlis was able to manifest Ba'al's corruption in a Dungeon and the entire reason for the Dungeon's existence. Omrak bent down, picking up the stone, and then turned to offer it to Asin at her yowl. She took it quickly, sliding it into a secure pocket inside her leather vest before the party moved on.

As they traversed more and more of the first floor, Daniel started offering more concrete directions as he guided the group through the floor. Each turn, each new cavern and passageway, was added to his mental map of the underground, a gift of his Mapping proficiency.

In a few hours and a few more Kobolds, the trio found the stairs down. Without a word, the party trooped down. The first floor held no challenges and, even worse, no coin to be earned.

***

The second floor was, as Liev warned, a significant contrast. Gone were stone hallways and narrow passages to be replaced by large wet grottos. Water dripped, ran, and pooled everywhere with only wet walkways treading through the cave. The group took a brief moment to register themselves on the portal stone before they carefully made their way forwards.

Bearing a lantern each, Omrak and Daniel slowly walked forwards, taking care with each step. Behind them, Asin rolled her eyes and let out a lazy yawn, her pupils wide as they drank in the meager light sources. Unlike the first floor, the party met their first attacker within minutes.

The Elemental Turtle surged out of the water and clamped its stone-infused jaws around Omrak's boot, taking them all by surprise. Omrak snarled, jumping away reflexively and shaking his foot in a futile attempt to detach the creature.

Howling, he put his foot down and readied his sword to cut the monster but is beaten to the act by Daniel, who'd anticipated Omrak's failure. Crouched low, Daniel swung his mace down hard, smashing the turtle on the shell hard enough to shatter it. Injured, the turtle opened its mouth to die a moment later as Daniel repeated his attack.

Pushing by Daniel, Asin huffed in anger as she picked up the only drop, a small Mana Stone. She looked at Omrak and then Daniel before she said, "No smash!"

Daniel offered a shrug in apology while Omrak inspected his foot, prodding at the bruised ankle. After he'd taken a tentative step, Omrak nodded to himself and stalked forwards as he paid closer attention to the water. Daniel's eyes narrowed as he gauged the damage from the slight hint of a limp that Omrak showed.

"Omrak, one second," he called out to the Northerner. Stepping forwards, he placed a hand on him and cast a quick Minor Healing. The spell wiped away a portion of the Barbarian's fatigue, his accumulated bruises, and the injured ankle.

"Ah!" Omrak drew a deep breath, the sudden absence of pain euphoric. "Your Healing is welcome if unnecessary. It was a minor injury."

"I doubt we'll get anything but minor injuries," Daniel said, glancing around. The turtles were annoying but, at their level, not dangerous. Not unless the group decided to have a nap at least.

"Very true, these are not ballad-worthy enemies," Omrak said, and Asin rolled her eyes. She turned her head, tracking the ripples in the water a distance away, her lips pulled apart to show glittering carnivorous teeth.

"Too far …" Daniel said, and Asin nodded. Still, she kept an eye on it as Omrak took off again.

"Let's map the place. Remember, our goal is the third floor," Daniel said, and the giant ahead of him rumbled agreement.

***

Fire turtles. Water turtles. Lightning turtles. Stone turtles. Air turtles, which were just strange with their tiny wings and their tendency to drop onto the party as an attack. Hours later, as they approached evening, Daniel was growing truly sick of turtles. The party had quickly developed a method of dealing with the monsters, but it did not make the repetition and annoyance any less.

Omrak had switched out his greatsword for his knife, using the pommel to smash apart turtles, or stabbing them in the guts after he flipped them over with his arms. Daniel's trusty mace was aptly suited for killing these monsters, and it was only Asin who lacked the brute strength or proper weaponry who found herself mostly ineffective. If not for her enchanted bracer that added small arcs of electricity to her attacks, she would have been rendered utterly ineffective. As it stood, Asin spent most of the level spotting for the two melee fighters.

On Omrak's back, his bag had begun to bulge with the Dungeon-created shells. Outside of a single, swirling, fire-patterned shell, all the others had been added to the pile. Asin kept that shell herself, intending to add it to her collection of rocks at home.

"Break?" Asin huffed as her stomach rumbled.

Looking around the cleared cavern, Daniel nodded and unslung his backpack, taking a seat near a rock a short distance from the water. The trio quickly took seats facing each other, allowing them to keep track of the cavern while they ate.

"You don't eat much, do you?" Daniel said, glancing at the wrapped sandwich that was dwarfed in Omrak's massive hands.

"Ah ..." Omrak said as he visibly hesitated.

Asin let out a huff before she picked up a small stone and tossed it at Daniel's head. Daniel flinched, and glared at his friend while she snorted and pulled apart part of her own sandwich, offering it to Omrak wordlessly.

"I could not ..."

"Eat," Asin growled, prodding him. "You fight."

Omrak stared at Asin, confused.

"She means you've been doing most of the fighting," Daniel clarified for Asin, who gave an appreciative nod.

"Ah ..." Omrak glanced at the offered sandwich again before he took it in his hand. "My thanks, Hero Asin."

When Omrak took a bite of the sandwich, his eyes widened, and he began puffing, his mouth wide open. Daniel choked off a laugh, realizing what had happened even as Omrak hastily drank from his waterskin.

"You are a true hero to eat that," Omrak said, eyes filled with admiration as he watched Asin continue to chew on her sandwich and spiced meat. Offering the half-eaten portion back to Asin, Omrak said, "I fear this challenge is beyond me."

"It is an acquired taste," Daniel said, eyes crinkling in humor. Asin just sniffed, though Daniel noted the lazily swinging tail that indicated her own amusement. Pulling apart his own sandwich, he traded with Omrak for the remains of the portion offered to him. "Tasty though when you've gotten used to it."

Omrak's eyes widened even further as he watched Daniel take a bite of the sandwich, the stocky Adventurer's only visible reaction a slight increase in mouth-breathing.

"Truly, I am in the company of great heroes."

***

"Floor guardian?" Omrak rumbled in question as they peered into the large cavern. Inside, a single Elemental Turtle sat, surveying its surroundings.

Its shell swirled in a pattern of red, gray, and their first white, indicating an attunement to fire, earth, and another element. The monster was twice the size of their previous opponents, just over four feet in length and a foot-and-a-half tall.

Elemental Turtle Champion (Level 4)
HP: 280/280

"Probably. See the stairs?" Daniel said, nodding past the Guardian to where a set of stairs led down.

"Yes. This should be a good fight," Omrak said as he sheathed his knife and pulled out his greatsword. Asin winced as he did so, Omrak having forgotten to keep his voice low as he had grown excited at the prospect of battle.

Turning its gaze to where the three hid, the Turtle let out a low roar accompanied by a surge of fire. The trio scurried backwards, hiding behind an outcropping till the flames died; Asin growling softly in displeasure at having lost the element of surprise.

The moment the fire died, Omrak charged from cover, screaming his own challenge. The Turtle counter-charged, at the last moment pulling its head back into its shell as it noted Omrak swinging at it. The sudden change in the monster's momentum made Omrak's attack fall short, the blow only landing at the edge of the blade and making a minor chip on the turtle's shell. The turtle's initial momentum unchecked, it knocked the barbarian off his feet, forcing the Northerner to flip over the shorter monster.

Behind Omrak, Daniel followed more carefully. Hunkered low, he engaged Double Strike, his own Skill Proficiency that made his mace blur as it smashed into the Turtle's shell. Each attack chipped away at the shell but left no other visible damage.

Hissing, the Turtle pulled itself out of its shell, snapping at Daniel. Daniel caught the attack low on his shield, stumbling slightly as he attempted to regain his balance from the low-angle of the attack. As the Turtle readied itself to bite again, a fan of throwing knives arrived, lightning sparking as they embedded themselves in the exposed body.

In pain, the Turtle snapped itself back into its shell and in doing so, knocking the knives free. Omrak's own swing, cutting horizontally, missed the legs and knocked the shell sideways, sending it spinning. For a moment, the Adventurers wondered if their eyes were playing tricks on them as the shell glowed with an inner white light.

Moving forwards cautiously, Daniel readied himself to continue the attack on the monster. When it popped its head out, Asin sent a knife at it, which was blocked by the monster charging forwards. Asin snarled slightly, readying another knife even as the Turtle opened its mouth to breathe fire again. Staring at the glowing mouth, Daniel ran sideways towards the water's edge and ducked low, covering his body with the shield even as the flames roared out.

Omrak, behind Daniel, took a more direct route, jumping over the attack. The barbarian swung his blade down, the greatsword cracking the shell with a loud clang of metal. To the side, Asin threw a Piercing Strike that drilled through the monster's leg, laming the Floor Champion.

The turtle roared in pain, glowing white as it struggled to heal the wounds. Water spilling from his body, Daniel ran from the shallows to lash out at the Turtle, who dodged by retracting into its body. Frustrated, Omrak tossed his sword aside and grabbed hold of the edge of the monster, flipping it over with a surge of strength.

Its soft under-belly exposed, both Asin and Daniel pummeled the monster with attacks, its healing factor unable to keep up. Omrak, having retrieved his sword, dealt the final blow by plunging his blade into the monster's exposed underbelly. Motes of blue light burst forth, dancing across the group before leaving the Champion's giant shell and a Mana Crystal.

The group panted in exhaustion, adrenaline slowly draining away. Daniel straightened before casting his Minor Healing on both Omrak and himself, fixing the accumulated injuries in the party. Omrak grinned, battle lust still riding high in his eyes, while Asin just shook her head. Being their only ranged attacker had its advantages.

After some searching, the group finally found the floor chest that the Champion was guarding. Within was the floor's Mana Crystal reward, a much larger and higher-grade crystal. As always, Asin pocketed the crystal for the group, her tail waving in happiness.

"Down?" Asin asked.

"Just to register ourselves," Daniel cautioned, and Asin nodded agreement. It was too late to start another floor.

***

Outside, after having registered themselves on the third-floor portal stone and transporting themselves back, the trio stretched. Daniel shared a friendly greeting with the new guards before the group walked towards the Guild Hall in good spirits. They had finished both floors in a single day!

"Omrak, are you going to need to fix your sword?" Daniel asked, recalling the massive blow that the Northerner had landed.

"No. Lund's Blessing is on my weapons," Omrak answered. At the raised eyebrow he received, Omrak explained. "It is a Skill Proficiency that increases the durability and strength of my weapons. My sword will not require fixing."

"Huh," Daniel said. As he considered Omrak's fighting style, Daniel could see how such a Skill Proficiency could be useful. He ran a finger along the edges of his mace, noting the deformed metal. Soon, he would have to look into either getting a new weapon or fixing this one. Luckily for Daniel, maces required significantly less care than swords. A blunt mace was still dangerous, after all.

Inside the Guild Hall, the group approached Liev when it was their turn. Asin quickly handed over their Mana Stones while Omrak proffered the bag of shells. Liev waved the group over to a nearby wider table so that he could properly assess their earnings. As Liev sorted and counted their earnings, muttering the totals of each item, both Asin and Omrak watched over the proceedings with rapt attention.

"Nine silver and four copper," announced Liev as he finished. Asin and Omrak both nodded immediately and then shared a long, considering look at each other. Daniel, on the other hand, had been watching the other Adventurers stream in, content to trust in his friends.

"That's a lot," he said. His first foray into the Karlak Dungeon had only netted him four silver from what he recalled.

"Yes. The Champion's shell is good quality and rare, and the Mana Stone you brought back is of slightly higher quality than previously," Liev said. Good as the haul was for the level, for a group of their size, the nine silver worked out to only three each. A decent but not special haul.

"We also made it to the third floor," Daniel added, curious to see if they needed a seal for that too.

"Really? Congratulations. I will inform the guards," Liev said. Normally he would have asked for some form of proof, but these two he trusted. After Liev had paid out the group, Asin sorted out the change before the group confirmed plans to test the third floor tomorrow.

Chapter 3

"This is a weird floor," Daniel muttered, pushing against the walls. The group stood just outside the portal room of the third level, poking and prodding at the walls and floor in confusion. The entire floor was built of a strange, flexible substance that reformed when pushed. In fact, the greater the force used to push against the walls, the faster the wall reformed. An experiment by Omrak had thrown him off his feet after he had punched the wall.

"Very strange," Asin hissed, her nose twitching. The entire floor smelled strange to her, a slightly acrid, sour smell that she had not encountered before. It made her fur stand up slightly and slowed the lazy, unconscious swinging of her tail.

"Asin, can you take the lead?" Daniel asked. Like his friend, he sensed something strange in this floor and wanted the Beastkin's better senses in front.

As Asin loped forwards, Daniel nodded for Omrak to follow along while he brought up the rear. What kind of monster took to living in a place like this?

The answer to that was as strange as the floor itself. Their first warning was the echoing squeaks of expelled air mixed with the sound of continuous collisions against the walls. The group tightened their formation, Daniel hefting his shield while Asin crouched low and to the side.

The noise culprit bounced around the corner at speed. A reflexive thrust by Omrak and a thrown knife by Asin both missed as the fast-moving monster pinged off one wall to the next. It slammed into Asin's shoulder, throwing the Catkin off balance, before bouncing to hit the flat of Omrak's blade to ricochet off the ceiling towards Daniel. Unable to dodge fully, Daniel bent his head low, letting the monster impact against his helmet. Most of the force was absorbed by the helmet, but it still made Daniel's neck ache.

As quickly as it had attacked, the monster was gone, bounding past the group. They straightened, staring at one another in confusion. None of them had managed to get a good look at the monster before it had left, leaving them even more puzzled.

A few minutes later, the trio were alerted to more incoming monsters. Asin crouched low again, her ears swiveling as she tracked the attackers, while the others got ready to fight. This time they were approached by a pair of the creatures, bouncing down the long hallway. Asin, tracking their movements, waited until the lead monster had bounced hard before she threw her knife. The Catkin snarled in anger, misjudging the speed, and tried again. This time, she managed to nick the monster, which let out an angry squeal.

Omrak waited till the nearest monster was within range before he swung, his greatsword whistling through the air and missing both monsters. The lead attacker caromed off a wall, slamming into Omrak's thigh and then his abdomen in short order before it hit the ceiling and rebounded back to attack Omrak again. The second monster ricocheted off the ground and slammed into Asin's stomach, bowling her over before it bounced to the ceiling and then Omrak's head, its new trajectory aimed directly at Daniel. Lightning danced when it hit Asin, but it seemed to do little to slow the creature.

Daniel, offered more time to set himself, launched a Shield Bash at the monster. The shield smashed into the monster, compressing the creature and sending it backwards towards Asin at speed. Asin flinched reflexively, raising the knife she held in her hand and accidentally impaled the fast-moving monster. Under the combined momentum, she collapsed backwards, staring at the dead monster held fast on her knife.

Omrak, finally fed up, reached out and grabbed the monster as it bounced on the barbarian's shoulder again. He snarled as the monster clamped teeth around his hand before he continued to crush the creature. Even with his Skill Proficiency of Lesser Strength Enhancement, the monster refused to die. In fact, the harder he squeezed, the harder it seemed to push back. With a yell, Omrak clamped a second hand around his own and exerted even more force, finally finding the hard core that made up the creature's internal body and crushing it.

Asin meanwhile stared at the impaled monster, a roughly spherical creature whose body felt very similar to the material of the walls around them. It had a series of small, tiny legs all around its body which it used to propel itself around, and as Omrak had found out, an inner, solid core.

Twinkin Sphere
HP: 0/27

The creatures finally broke up into motes of light, leaving behind Mana cores and a sliver of their stretchy skin.

"So … that happened," Daniel finally said into the silence.

***

"Head's up!" Daniel shouted, swinging his mace with full force at the bouncing monster hours later. Struck, the monster compressed and flew backwards towards Omrak, who shifted the angle of his blade slightly, letting the monster split itself apart on the edge of his sword.

To Daniel's left, Asin threw a Piercing Shot that drilled and pinned another Sphere to the wall. It struggled for a moment before finally expiring, breaking up completely. The third monster bounced off Daniel's shoulder, bruising him before getting away.

Chuckling to himself, Daniel rubbed at his shoulder through his armor while the others regrouped. After hours of wandering the third floor, the group had learnt three things. Firstly, there were no traps in this Dungeon. Second, it was rare for the Twinkin Spheres to hang out after its initial attack. Lastly, while attacks came regularly, the monsters did not seem to be able to do much damage with each attack.

"Shall we go?" Daniel asked, and at Asin's nod, they continued to move deeper into the Dungeon. A short few minutes and a pair of attacks later, the group found themselves overlooking their first true cavern on the floor. They gaped at the numerous columns that dotted the floor and snaked upwards while a small, steep path led down to the cavern floor. In a corner, they could see another staircase, leading down to the fourth floor. Flickering in the low light of the Mana-imbued walls, the group noticed scores of the Twinkin Spheres bouncing around, smashing into columns and each other with wild abandon. Dotted throughout the cavern were more exits, leading to different locations. Occasionally, Spheres would bounce into or exit those entrances.

"We have to get down," muttered Daniel.

"Dangerous," Asin said.

"Aye, a single hit is nothing for Heroes like us. But on that trail and with that many …" Omrak rumbled. Daniel blinked, looking at the barbarian. Well, it seemed he did have a cautious bone in his body. "Still, a hero can only go forward. I shall lead the way."

Or not.

"Uhhh …" Daniel said, cudgeling his brain for a better plan.

"Rope," Asin said, already unslinging her backpack. Daniel nodded quickly in agreement. It only took them a few moments before the trio had roped themselves together. As an additional precaution, they tied another rope to a nearby column and looped the ropes they tied on themselves to it. A last knot at the end of the rope gave them some additional safety before they tossed the ropes down the entrance.

"Come, we shall reap a whirlwind of …" Omrak paused, staring outwards. "Spheres."

"Go." Asin prodded the giant who shifted away from the sharp claw.

Exiting the cavern, the trio slowly edged their way down to the cavern floor, eyes alert. The Twinkin Spheres at first seemed oblivious to their descent but soon the trio saw a change in their movements. More and more monsters began angling towards them. Curling up slightly behind his shield, Daniel growled as he readied for the fight. Ahead, Omrak had switched weapons to his large knife, wielding it in his left hand while the right gripped the rope. Asin pulled her melee knives as well, ready to defend herself as the monsters closed in.

Daniel took the first few attacks on his shield, letting each monster bounce off it into the darkness. His mace was pretty much useless as a weapon against these monsters, and so, he could only guard himself as they edged down. Asin twisted and ducked, slashing at passing monsters and occasionally taking a blow to her body. Omrak, the largest of the trio, was beaten black and blue by the bouncing creatures even as he swung his knife in mostly futile swipes.

"Keep moving!" Daniel shouted through the storm of noise as the Spheres assaulted them. Under the deluge of monsters that started arriving in greater and greater numbers, Omrak missed Daniel's shout and began to focus on defense and attack, coming to a complete stop.

Asin, smaller and lighter than both, curled up closer to the wall. Knives held in her hands, the

Catkin swung at any movement she spotted even as arcs of electricity danced all around her as the monsters struck her and her enchanted aura. Growling as she grew increasingly bruised, Asin slapped the gorget and the rune on it, activating the Shield spell. It flared into light, her aura strengthened such that the monsters bounced off it before impacting her. Given a brief respite from the attacks, Asin stood and started throwing knives, engaging her Skill Proficiency, Fan of Knives to give Omrak a brief moment of relief too.

Omrak, having realized the futility of standing and fighting had already begun edging his way down. In the gap created by Asin's knives, the Northerner rushed down. Keeping a hand up to protect his face, he hurried down the pathway, almost tripping on his feet in his haste. Each blow seemed to draw a deeper red glow from his body that spread outwards, his movements growing more sure. On the ground, the barbarian drew his sword, the weapon dancing as it sliced apart Twinkin Spheres, a wide grin appearing on Omrak's face.

Behind, Asin quickly slipped past Daniel to make her way to the bottom of the cavern to take station slightly behind Omrak. In the safety of his larger form, Asin cut at the monsters that Omrak missed before they could bounce away again. Daniel was the last to arrive, hunkered down behind his shield as he was. Once on the floor, he took station to Omrak's left, providing his meager support by blocking attacks from one side. Of the three, his greater degree of armor and shielding ensured that he was the least hurt.

"How many are there?" Daniel gasped.

"One. Two. Many!" Asin snarled, pinning another Sphere.

"COME. FACE ME. I AM OMRAK, SON OF LOSIN," shouted Omrak as he whirled his sword around him. Out of the corner of his eyes, Omrak saw something larger flying through the air, a sphere the size of Daniel's shield. Before Omrak could attack it, the humongous Twinkin Sphere slammed the barbarian off his feet.

"Champion," Asin snapped, and Daniel nodded, bending down to cover Omrak as he laid a hand on the Northerner. Cracked ribs, bruised muscles, and a bit lip was what Daniel sensed with his Gift almost immediately. He grunted as he pulled his Gift back, even as the memory of his latest bread recipe slipped from his mind as payment. A Minor Healing would fix up Omrak.

Before Daniel was able to cast the spell, Omrak surged to his feet with a roar. His eyes bloodshot, red light leaking from his body, the Northerner scanned for the monster, idly slicing apart an attacking Sphere. Already, the combined efforts of the trio had reduced the monster numbers significantly, such that attacks came only occasionally.

"There!" Daniel said as he spotted the bouncing Champion.

Omrak shifted, his sword ready as the Champion lined itself up for an attack. Disregarding Omrak, it bounced towards Asin, only to be intercepted by Daniel, who Shield Bashed the monster backwards to Omrak. The momentum was so great that Daniel felt the muscles and tendons of his shoulder tear slightly. It was not for naught as Omrak speared the Champion on his greatsword, ending its life. Soon after that the group cleared the cavern and retrieved all the stones, before they hurried down to the next level.

In the safety of the foyer of the fourth floor, the group rested. Daniel groaned, casting Healer's

Mark on all three of them before casting Minor Healing again on Omrak, who was the most gravely wounded. His work as the group's healer complete, Daniel sighed, resting against the wall as he waited for the healing spells to take effect. Already, he noted how large a drop he had experienced in his Mana from these simple spells.

While the group waited, Daniel glanced at the notification on his screen and his full Status Screen.

Skill Level Up

Club Skill has increased to Novice level. +5% damage for all club-based weapons.

Name: Daniel Chai

Class: Level 7 Adventurer (31%)

Sub-classes: Level 7 (Miner) (14%)

Human (Male)

Statistics

Life: 243

Stamina: 243

Mana: 177

Attributes

Strength: 23

Agility: 21

Constitution: 29

Intelligence: 18

Willpower: 18

Luck: 14

Skills

Unarmed Combat: Level 3 (38/100)

Clubs (Novice): Level 1 (04/100)

Archery: Level 2 (48/100)

Shield: Level 9 (44/100)

Dodge: Level 6 (19/100)

Combat Sense: Level 7 (03/100)

Perception: Level 6 (77/100)

Mining: Level 7 (78/100)

Healing: Level 9 (44/100)

Herb Lore: Level 3 (31/100)

Stealth: Level 2 (14/100)

Cooking: Level 3 (89/100)

Singing: Level 2 (14/100)

Skill Proficiencies

Double Strike

Shield Bash

Perin's Blow

Mapping (II)

Spells

Minor Healing (I)

Healer's Mark (I)

Gifts

Martyr's Touch—The caster may heal oneself or others by touch and concentration, sacrificing a portion of his life to do so. Cost varies depending on the extent of the injuries healed.

Not as good as a Level Up but he would take it, thought Daniel. Beside him, as their wounds healed, his party members also regarded their own notifications.

"More?" Asin asked, after the group finally looked away from their notifications.

"I am willing," Omrak said, stretching.

"No, let's go back," Daniel said. "We've got a bunch of stones and it's getting late. I'm also nearly out of Mana so if there's something out there …"

"Level Four!" Asin pointed out.

"Yeah … and that was a Level Three. We didn't have the right equipment. We're doing great, Asin," Daniel argued back, while Omrak watched quietly.

Asin stared grumpily at Daniel before she turned to Omrak. "Vote!"

"Let us continue. I yearn to see what comes next," Omrak rumbled, and Asin flashed a grin at Daniel. The stocky Adventurer just sighed and waved them towards the entrance. Well, it certainly looked like they would be checking out the next Level.

***

"Crossbow?" Asin asked, staring upwards as they stood under the Dungeon sky. And sky it was, for there were even clouds that floated above along with birds. It was the birds that Asin watched, their long and sharp talons glinting. Standing in the exit, she drew a deep breath, tasting the scents in the air. Even now, underground, it smelled of fresh air and grass, trees and flowers. Even a wind ruffled her fur.

"Didn't bring it," Daniel said, and Omrak shook his head in turn.

"Net. Bow," Asin muttered to herself, and Omrak had to nod in agreement. It seemed that a net to catch the fast-moving monsters or a bow to kill them at a distance would soon be added to the list of things a Karlak Adventurer required. It certainly would be a boon for the city's merchants.

"I fear we must turn back. We are not equipped for this," Omrak rumbled, and Asin reluctantly nodded. As much as she wanted to check out the floor in more detail, she was now outvoted.

"Well, at least we made it this far," Daniel consoled the group as they retreated back to the foyer and exited the Dungeon. Reaching the fourth floor in only two days was quite good, especially considering the fact that the Dungeon itself only had ten floors maximum as a Beginner Dungeon. As they exited, Asin shot one last, longing look over her shoulder.

Chapter 4

"Daniel. Asin. Omrak," greeted Liev as the trio walked to his counter. He raised an eyebrow as Omrak turned, dropping his backpack on the table. Like the Dungeon, the Adventurers' Guild had seen a minor transformation as well. Gone were the chest-high counters that the attendants had worked from. Instead, tables had replaced the counters with sufficient space for Adventurers to deposit their loot. Unlike the old Karlak Dungeon, the new Dungeon seemed to excel at providing additional drops.

"Is it worth anything?" Daniel asked as Liev examined the Twinkin Sphere skin.

"Mmmm … we can offer you a copper per five skins," Liev said at last, putting the skin back on the counter. Asin hissed at that, her eyes narrowing in distrust. "This is a new loot drop. Until we learn more about what potential uses it might have, the purchase is purely speculative."

Asin growled again while Omrak just shrugged phlegmatically.

"Asin, do you want to keep this? Maybe once they know what it is …?" Daniel asked.

The Catkin snarled at Daniel before catching herself, staring at the pieces before she nodded in reluctant acceptance. Omrak scooped up the pieces and stuffed them back into his bag, clearing the table for Asin to deposit the Mana Stones. When Liev reached the large Mana Stones from the Champion and the floor chest, he stopped and raised a bushy red eyebrow.

"Did you find the stairway down?" Liev said.

"Yes, we're registered for the fourth floor," Daniel said proudly.

"Very good! I do believe that makes you the first group to get that far," Liev said, smiling slightly. "Well done."

"Your thanks are appreciated, Attendant Halliope," Omrak said. Daniel blinked, trying to recall where he had heard that name before. After a moment, he dismissed it. He had probably heard someone else call Liev by his family name at some point. It might even be a fragment left behind by his Gift. It was uncommon, but occasionally his Gift took fragments of a memory rather than complete sections.

"You should look at the quest board then. We just posted it today," Liev said, smiling at the group as he finished counting their earnings. The pile of coin he pushed forwards was significantly smaller than yesterday's, which made Asin grimace as she divvied up the amount.

"Thanks, Liev, we will," Daniel said, waving goodbye to the redhead attendant as he walked over to the board. He did not need to ask which quest Liev had directed him to, for the posting dominated the board.

Dungeon Completion

The Adventurers' Guild of Karlak has authorized a one-time payment of 50 Gold for the completion of the newly reorganized Karlak Beginner Dungeon. This is an open request available to all parties. quest completion will be ascertained via the delivery of the Dungeon Boss's Mana Stone.

Daniel read the notice before Omrak's insistent elbow made him read it out loud. Omrak sucked in a breath on hearing the quest reward.

"I could buy a farm ..." Omrak muttered to himself.

"Farm?" Asin and Daniel's harmonious cry of incredulity made Omrak look at them puzzled.

"Yes. The farm next to my father's would be suitable," said Omrak. Thinking back, he continued, "It lies on good earth and is fed by the same river as my father's. The family needs more land. I believe we shall dedicate a third of it to cattle. The market for good beef is always strong."

Daniel just continued to stare at the teenaged giant next to him, trying to imagine the muscular, shirtless barbarian pulling up weeds. Asin worked her jaw for a moment before she finally shook her head, prodding Daniel to make him shut his mouth. Omrak was oblivious to their reactions as he continued to detail his ideal farm.

"… and Greel can collect the shit!" roared Omrak with laughter at a joke that only he could understand.

"Oy! Shut it," called another Adventurer, to whom Omrak bobbed his head in acknowledgement.

"Safe to say we're going to try for it?" Daniel said, filling in the silence. He knew he had no need to ask Asin. It was more likely for her to turn down a meal than a chance to earn more coin. Especially as the quest coincided with something they were already doing.

"Yes!" Omrak nodded again, Asin inclining her head in agreement as her tail lashed out behind her in excitement.

As Daniel opened his mouth to continue, a commotion in the Guild entrance drew their attention. A party of four Adventurers strode in. The first wore full plate armor, his face covered by a helmet. Dirt and dust from the road caked the armor, dulling its shine, but Daniel could tell it was of high quality almost immediately by the lack of noise as the fighter moved. Behind him, a scarred older man walked, his shoulders broader than Omrak's but a few inches shorter than the youngster. The older man carried the largest pack of all, his body bowed slightly under the weight. Following the pair, a bookish younger man walked, looking around with a studied air while a last, shorter, and quieter fighter brought up the rear.

"Mage," Asin growled softly.

"How ...?" said Daniel.

"Pouches." Asin gestured to the belt and Daniel looked, finally spotting the indicated items.

"I don't ..."

"Mages must carry their spell components with them. The numerous pouches are often a giveaway," rumbled Omrak.

"Oh …" Daniel shook his head, still uncertain about the reasons for this.

"Mana less. Crushed crystal expensive," Asin explained.

Daniel blinked, nodding. Healing magic never needed a catalyst—the bodies they worked with were the catalyst that was used. When cast, the Spell took a small portion of the healthy body as the template and developed from there. It was why illnesses that degraded the whole body or old age were nearly impossible to cure—the Healer had no template to work from and had to substitute their own Mana. While a good Healer might slow the aging process using just Mana, it was to such a low degree that most did not bother.

Mages who were attempting to alter the very fabric of nature would need to carry a catalyst of some form to start the process. A crushed Mana Stone, which was basically pure Mana, could be substituted, but of course, was expensive. What Daniel had not known was that other reagents could be used. After all, Daniel had never met a Mage in-person before.

Lost in thought, Daniel missed the rest of the entrance of the group. When the stocky Adventurer started paying attention again, he was surprised to note that the plate-mail-clad fighter was a brunette female who had stowed her helmet under one arm.

"We just came from Silverstone. What do you mean you can't let us in till tomorrow!" the woman demanded, her voice cultured and smooth. Around her, the Guild had fallen silent as everyone listened in.

"I'm sorry, but Guild rules are clear. Every group must take their turn on entry. As tomorrow is the last day of the group entrances, I can fit you in then. But not a moment earlier," Liev said, entirely calm.

"This is ridiculous. We will finish your Dungeon in a week!" she snapped, her hands pressing down on the table. "Let us in and get this done and we'll be gone."

The warrior woman either ignored or was oblivious to the indrawn breath and hisses her bold statement caused among the other Adventurers. The shorter party member at the rear, though, was not, hunching lower as he squirmed in embarrassment.

"Amrah, this is sufficient," the scrawny Mage said. "I would prefer to rest anyway."

The brunette warrior turned, glaring at the Mage, but then deflated. "Fine. Get us a token for tomorrow then, attendant. Make it out to the Crimson Elms."

When the group finally left, the Guild Hall broke into excited babbling.

"Advanced party?" Daniel asked Asin and Omrak, knowing in his heart that they were.

"Yes."

"It is clear."

"Damn …" Daniel sighed, looking towards the quest reward. Their chances of winning it was now gone. They stood no chance against an Advanced team. Asin followed his gaze before she shrugged, tapping her coin pouch as she eyed the deepening sun.

"Dungeon tomorrow?" Asin asked to confirm plans.

"I fear I might not be able to acquire such equipment as necessary by tomorrow," Omrak rumbled. "It is late."

"We can skip the nets for now," said Daniel, staring into the distance. "You don't use a bow or crossbow, do you?"

"No. It is not traditional for my people. I am well versed in the throwing axe, though I lack one," Omrak said.

"Not a problem; I know someone who probably stocks some." Daniel grinned and said to Asin. "We'll get going then."

Asin nodded, before she waved goodbye to the pair, who immediately headed out of the doorway.

***

A short while later, the pair of Adventurers were banging on the door of Max's shop.

"He's a very good armorer. Also carries some weapons, though he doesn't specialize in it. We did a quest for him not so long ago so he kind of likes us," explained Daniel to Omrak.

"Some of us like to sleep," the armorer and weaponsmith grumbled as he dragged open the bar across his door. "If it weren't for you, Daniel ..."

"I know. I know. I've got news for you though," Daniel said as he stepped in, while Max wandered around the shop lighting the lanterns. Omrak walked in, his eyes drinking in the displays of armor and weapons he could never have afforded.

"Well, out with it!" grumbled Max.

"We managed to make it to Level Four! Now, on Level Three there's these weird monsters called Twinkin Spheres ..." Daniel immediately launched into an explanation of the monsters. Max nodded, listening as he stroked his beard in thought. Behind them, Omrak perused the store, searching for a suitable weapon.

"... so we were thinking it'd be nice to have a net. For all three levels. They'd catch the turtles and fish them out, grab the Spheres and we could even use them against the birds," finished Daniel.

"And they'll need to be weighted," muttered Max, and nodded. "We can make that. Simple work, in fact."

Omrak cried out, pulling forth a pair of throwing axes in their sheaths from a weapon rack near the back of the shop. Grinning, the large Barbarian held up the pair to Max.

"How much for this, Master Tradesman?"

"That'd be two silver for you," Max said. "And before you ask, that's as low as I'll go."

Omrak nodded, pulling the sheath off the head of one and looking at the edge. He frowned slightly, turning it side to side before checking the next one. "This is not your work."

"No. Apprentice work. Good enough to sell, though."

"Aye, but not as fine as your other equipment." Omrak hefted the axes one last time before he slid them into their sheaths. Hefting his pouch, Omrak turned to Max, "Two silver is fair."

"Good. You going to change out that mace of yours anytime soon, Daniel?" Max asked, glancing at the battered weapon by the stocky Adventurer's side. "Seen better days."

"Mmm … not yet."

"Well, let me know when you're ready. Now shoo! Some of us have lives."

Chuckling, the pair quickly exited the shop soon after, parting ways as they left.

***

In the Clinic, Daniel stretched. After a hard day's dungeon delving, most others would be taking a break. For Daniel, as he had a little Mana left and a girlfriend who worked at the Clinic, he found himself finishing up his day in the small examination room and office.

"You need to eat more than potatoes," Daniel sighed, waving a finger at the muscular man before him. "Meat. Fruit. Have a stew once in a while."

"But I don't like anything else," the large man whined.

"Then you'll continue to be tired. Can't do anything for you," Daniel said, pointing to the door. "Your body isn't getting what it needs. Eat properly."

Daniel watched the man leave glumly and shook his head. It bothered him that he could feel the deficiency in the man's body with his Gift, but he had no idea what it was. Last winter, he had seen quite a few of these cases, which led him to believe it had to do with the reduced food types available to his patients. Even with the combined knowledge offered by the Elves and

Dwarves, there was much that they still did not understand. He often felt like he was blindly subscribing cures because they worked, without understanding the why.

As the door opened, Daniel shook his head and focused on his new patient. Another patient who had waited too long before visiting, ensuring that a simple cut was now infected. Grunting, Daniel reached for the basin of water to clean the wound. Having wiped away dirt, pus and blood to see the cut properly, Daniel cast Healer's Mark on the man.

"Wait outside; don't touch the wound. It'll heal in an hour. When it's healed, you can leave," Daniel said, a slight headache reminding him that he was close to running out of Mana.

"I have to …"

"Don't. Leave," Daniel snapped, fixing the man with a glare. The laborer looked at the large, stocky Healer before him and remembered that as nice as he was, he was also an Adventurer. Dealing with a stubborn laborer would not be a problem for him.

"Yes sir!"

Daniel rubbed his forehead and washed his hands as the man left. Maybe he should have just washed it down with Dwarven Whisky. It normally worked. However, the stubborn idiot probably would never come back if it did not. Even before his breath had caught, the door opened again with another patient.

***

"You look like you could use a night's sleep." Khy'ra's voice floated to Daniel's ears as he sat quietly, eyes closed. As he opened his eyes, Daniel realized that he had actually been sleeping for a bit.

"Sorry. Long day," Daniel said. "The patients …?"

"Are gone. Sent them home for today." Khy'ra walked over, grabbing his arm and then wrinkling her nose. "What is that smell?"

"Twinkin Spheres. Level Three monster. Very strange …"

"Huh. Bath house first then," Khy'ra said, pulling Daniel up with one hand. "Come on, you can tell me all about it there."

Later, in a private room in the bath house, Daniel stared at the delivered plate of food. He poked at it, glancing over to his girlfriend before he asked, "I didn't realize they let you eat in here."

"It helps if the owner owes you one," Khy'ra said, arching her back slightly as she dug fingers into her lower back. "Ugh …"

"Here, let me do that," Daniel said, pulling her over to help and copping a quick feel. Khy'ra snorted, shaking her head, but relaxed into his strong fingers.

"Can you afford this, though? A private room is expensive," Daniel said, glancing around.

"It's fine."

Daniel fell silent, working the knots out of her lower back. This display alongside the continued existence of the Clinic once again made him wonder exactly how successful an Adventurer Khy'ra had been before she retired. While he knew that she received funds from the City and other donors, he doubted it was sufficient. And if Khy'ra lived a mostly austere life, her occasional indulgences seemed to be particularly spectacular.

"Thinking again," Khy'ra said, interrupting Daniel's musing. "You should be eating before it gets cold."

"Yeah, sorry." Rather than admit his actual thoughts, Daniel said, "We had an Advanced team arrive today. They'll probably take the Dungeon clear quest."

"Why?"

"Probably for the quest."

"Why do you think they'll win?"

"They're an Advanced team," Daniel said, frowning. It was obvious, was it not?

"And …?"

"They've got more experience than we do! Better equipment, better Skills," Daniel said, exasperated.

"Not necessarily. And it's not all important."

"I don't understand."

"Think about it, Daniel. Would a high-level Advanced group travel all the way to just complete a Beginner Dungeon? How much did that Advanced Group you worked with make in one day on the first floor?"

Daniel opened his mouth and then shut it, thinking back to his visit to Silvestone. She was right, Nico and his party had only completed Peel because it was on their way. They would not have traveled to Karlak just to complete the Dungeon. The experience bonus and the earnings, even with the quest, would not have been worth the travel time.

"They're still an Advanced Group …"

"That just means they've completed a Beginner Dungeon," Khy'ra said. "The difference between a Beginner Adventurer and a new Advanced Adventurer isn't that great. Not like it is for the gap between Advanced and Expert. And don't forget, a party is more than their levels. It's the Skills and the teamwork that matter."

"You think we can complete the quest?"

"I don't know. And neither do you."

"Oh …" Daniel blinked. Khy'ra as always was right. It was annoying sometimes dating a couple-of-hundred-years-old Elf who had seen it all before.

"Daniel …" The Elf frowned, staring at the young man before she shook her head.

"What?"

"Never mind."

"What?"

"Why are you an Adventurer?" Khy'ra finally asked.

Caught off guard by the question, Daniel paused in silence as he tried to find the answer to that. 'Because I wanted to be' was not really a good answer. Neither was 'I didn't want to be a Healer or Miner'. Neither really spoke to why he wanted to be an Adventurer in particular. Brow furrowed, he tried to work out a proper answer for Khy'ra, who nibbled on the dishes while she waited.

"Well … I guess I wanted to see the world," Daniel finally said.

"Mmm … so why not be a questor?" Khy'ra asked. Questors were Adventurers who specialized in fulfilling quests. They rarely, if ever, entered Dungeons.

"I don't like quests. They are boring," Daniel said. "It's the same thing, all the time. There's no... thrill, no danger."

Khy'ra laughed, shaking her head. "And that makes you a true Adventurer. But what do you want from it?"

"Well … I …" Daniel paused as he attempted to find a reply.

"Perhaps something to think about for later. Now, let's eat before the tub gets too cold!" Khy'ra said, pushing a plate towards Daniel. She knew better than to push him, not now.

Chapter 5

"Good balance," Asin said as she watched the borrowed throwing axe embed itself in the tree. Inside the Dungeon on the fourth floor, the group had taken a short stop to allow Omrak a chance to refresh his throwing Skills. Nearby, Daniel sat with his crossbow knocked, clad only in the helmet, breastplate, shoulder pauldrons, and bracers of his plate armor, watching the skies for potential trouble. Thus far, none of the birds had come close.

Unlike other floors, this one seemed to stretch forever, a single trail leading forwards through the plains. Daniel knew that much of this was illusion—that there was a definite wall in the distance and all around them, but the illusion was so convincing, he struggled not to accept it. As the wind rustled the grass, he stared at the scrawny tree that the pair had taken to punishing.

"We done yet?" Daniel asked impatiently.

"I believe I have regained most of my former skill. Let us seek glory!" Omrak replied, his voice a roar. Asin, next to him, winced, edging away.

"Don't go too far, Asin, we'll need to cover each other," Daniel said as they started to walk forwards. Asin just left in a huff, though she slowed down to let the pair close in. Hefting the extra quiver of crossbow bolts over his shoulder, Daniel followed along.

"You wear only part of your armor today, Hero Daniel," Omrak mentioned as he walked alongside.

"Figured it'd be easier to move without the leg armor," said Daniel.

"Truth. I find great freedom in not having armor," said Omrak.

"I thought you couldn't afford it."

"That too," Omrak replied cheerfully.

***

A few minutes later, as the group followed the path, Daniel spotted the first sign of trouble. A trio of the birds had started winging their way towards them. He hefted his crossbow, waiting. He knew he was a poor shot, so he had no intention of firing early.

Ahead of him, Asin had stopped and drawn a single throwing knife. She sniffed, tasting the air as she waited for Daniel to shoot first. Omrak absently flipped his own throwing axe in his hand, being relegated to the last attacker. After all, he only had two hatchets, so losing or breaking them was a serious concern.

The trio watched the birds wing their way to them, getting closer and closer. Wide wingspans, a long-hooked beak, and sharp talons that glinted kept the three watching. Just as Daniel raised his crossbow to aim at them, they turned and flew away, circling the group as they climbed high above the trio.

"Weird," muttered Daniel. He could not think of a monster that actually refused to attack.

"Go?" Asin asked after they watched the birds circle for a few minutes with no sign of coming down.

"I guess," Daniel said. He could possibly hit one of them, but he really did not trust his aim. He could still remember missing stationary tree trunks a short few months ago. For that matter, he'd never tried to shoot directly into the sky before.

The group started walking again, occasionally looking upwards at the circling birds. Not long later, a pair of birds winged over as well. Again, the group set themselves, and again, the birds winged away before the trio could attack them.

Joining the initial three, the new pair continued to circle the Adventurers.

For another uneventful hour, the party continued to trudge the Dungeon level, unmolested. Twice more, birds winged towards them before finally joining the group above, circling the trio. In time, the group found themselves craning their neck upwards constantly, trying to discern what was happening and wary of attack by the large number above them.

"Horses," rumbled Omark.

"Uhh …" Daniel frowned, tilting his head to the side. He heard nothing in the wind.

"I feel the trembling in the earth. Many horses," Omrak said.

"Not horses," Asin said, exhaling with a huff. "Something ground."

"Ground …" Eyes wide, Daniel squatted and placed a hand on the ground. He hissed, looking around desperately. "That's a Tremqua Worm!"

"I know not this monster," Omrak said, staring at the ground intently as if, by sheer force of will alone, he could see through it. "How do we fight it?"

"You don't," snapped Daniel. Nothing, no rocky outcroppings, no solid earth. He cast his mind back, eyeing his minimap and then snapped, "This way!"

Daniel took off at a run, leading the group to his new destination. His friends rushed along behind him, Asin quickly catching up and loping alongside. Instead of speaking, she kept her breath for the sprint. As they ran, the trembling grew in strength such that even Daniel could feel it through his reinforced, solid boots.

The group burst into the clearing of gravel that Daniel recalled seeing, only stopping when they were a good ten feet in. Breath heaving, Daniel eyed the ground as he spoke between breaths, hands still flexing around his crossbow. "The Worms travel deep underground until they are ready to attack. Then they surface. That's when they are most dangerous. If we survive that, they'll travel just below the surface until we kill them."

"Why are we here?" Omrak asked, staring warily at his feet as the rumbling increased.

Asin's ears perked up, her hand to the ground as she attempted to sense where the monster would erupt from. Daniel swayed lightly on the balls of his feet as he answered, "They're so large that it takes a while for what they eat to expel. If they eat the rock, it slows them down. A bit."

Daniel was sweating, his breathing slightly faster than normal. Asin, having seen the unusual distress her friend was in, called out, "How know?"

"What?"

"Worm. Know?"

"I fought them as a Miner," Daniel said. "My … we …" Memories of his father, of waiting and waiting for a man who never came back. And the story that came out later of a Tremqua Worm attack. It had been the worst attack the Mine had experienced in ages, one that killed a half-dozen Miners.

Daniel shivered, his mind wandering as he was caught up in old memories. He did not notice the change in vibrational speed that indicated the monster was close. Asin realized her error with a start and dashed over, tackling Daniel a moment before the monster burst from the ground. The Tremqua Worm looked much like a normal earthworm, segmented body and a wide mouth that swallowed the earth as it lunged upwards.

Unlike an earthworm, though, its body was as thick around as Omrak's waist.

The smaller Catkin was unable to move Daniel aside in sufficient time completely, the Tremqua Worm gripping and ripping part of his leg off. Daniel screamed in pain even as the monster twisted in the air, arching its body to fall towards the pair of tangled Adventurers. It slammed into Asin's back, only a last-minute activation of her Shield rune stopping the monster from ripping a hole through her back. The Catkin whimpered as the force of the blow compressed her chest even under the protection of the rune. Unable to pierce her defense, the Worm began to dig along the ground to escape.

Omrak roared, charging towards the pair and swinging his sword at the exposed segment. It took the giant of a man a single swing, muscles flexing as the blade parted the monster's body in half. Omrak howled in glee, using the momentum of his blade to slice again at the portion of body left behind as it still squirmed. The top half fled into the ground, squirming away before Asin could twist around to attack it.

Daniel was curled up on the ground, hands clamped down on his injured calf to slow the flow of blood as he cast Minor Healing. The first spell scabbed the wound over, after which he cast Healer's Mark before he pushed himself to his feet. The crossbow banged on his thigh as he stood up, ignored by Daniel in favor of his mace.

"Where is it?" he snarled, realizing he had not even taken off his shield. Now, he had not the time to do so.

"There." Asin pointed with one hand, holding the other above her head ready to throw her knife. Omrak continued to slice and kick the half of the Worm that still squirmed, intent on killing it.

Daniel watched as the monster twisted, coming around to where he stood. Struck by a sudden thought, he waited patiently till the monster was nearly on him before he jumped and swung his mace into the ground while activating his Skill Proficiency Perin's Blow.

The attack doubled the strength of his strike, passing through the earth to the monster. It injured the Worm, making the monster swirl away. Daniel snarled, taking a step forwards and triggering another Perin's Blow immediately, but only managing to catch the end of the monster, making it change direction again.

Daniel was distracted from his obsession with the Worm by a pained yowl. Asin had a deep cut along one shoulder, her other hand waving a knife against the birds that were dive-bombing her. Before Daniel could take this in fully, he realized that a bird was coming at him. He threw himself to the side too late, claws screeching against his breastplate from the failed attack. Omrak fared the best of all as he ignored the attacks, preferring to return hurt for hurt. When bird met blade, bird lost spectacularly.

Asin rolled and came up with a pair of blades in her hands before she threw them at the birds, engaging Fan of Blades. Each blade exploded into multiples, spinning through the air. Most missed, unaimed as they were, but some hit and offered Asin more time to continue her attacks.

Daniel, relieved that his armor was sufficient to ward him for the moment, refocused on locating the Worm.

"Omrak. Move!" Daniel roared as he charged forwards, desperate to save his friend. Omrak danced aside, moving his feet as he swung his sword above him. Already, red mist filled the air around Omrak as he took more and more damage. With another roar, Omrak buried his sword in the ground a moment too soon to decapitate the Worm. Unable to stop, the Worm smashed into the buried metal and squirmed to get around it.

Daniel, finally caught up, swung his mace again, triggering Perin's Blow one last time. The attack left a deep depression in the ground as the monster was crushed, earth churning as it died. Crouched low, Daniel looked up to see that Omrak was guarding him from further attacks from the birds as he swung his blade around to his own detriment. Blood flowed from open wounds, deep cuts along his torso including a few inches of flesh that hung loose from his shoulder.

Eyes narrowed, Daniel reached out and cast Healer's Mark on Omrak. Already, Daniel could see the blood flow slowing. Turning his head to the side, he spotted Asin continuing to attack the quintuplet of birds that targeted her, her movements as graceful as always as she danced away from them. Still, the Catkin was bleeding from a dozen minor wounds including a scrape along one cheek.

No longer distracted, the group focused on dealing with the attacking birds. Daniel even found time to recock his crossbow and fire it.

Once. And miss. Both Omrak and Asin dealt with the flying monsters quickly, injuring wings and sending the birds crashing to the ground.

Panting, Asin gripped her shoulder where she had wrenched it accidentally. Behind the Catkin, her tail swung lazily, belying her ragged state. "Bad shot."

"Keep laughing and I won't heal you," Daniel threatened as he walked over, his own wound finally healed.

Asin stuck her tongue out as Daniel placed his hand on her shoulder, casting Healer's Mark. Turning around, Daniel spotted Omrak, who was busy digging into the earth for the Mana Stone.

"Tough," Asin said, her moment of humor gone.

"The monsters? Alone … maybe not. But together …" Daniel shook his head. He definitely felt he had made a mistake not wearing his full suit of armor.

"A glorious fight," Omrak said, grinning. "Blood and feathers. All around."

Asin snorted before she pointed to the way they came and tilted her head to the side. Daniel blinked, glancing backwards and then at Omrak.

Either choice they made, it was unlikely they would finish the level this day.

Chapter 6

"Temqua Worms and Grish Raptors," Liev said as he wrote down the information the group provided. "Working together too. Very interesting."

After their first fight, the trio decided to retreat the entrance before wandering in an elaborate circle to draw additional Temqua Worms. Interestingly enough, unlike other levels, the fourth level had few attacks and the group only had a chance to test their Skills out twice more before they called it a day.

"Good-sized stones, though," Liev said, tapping the trio of large Mana Stones that he had set apart. "C-grade eights and nines are very good for the level. Of course, the Raptors are only D-grade tens, so it balances out."

"No drops," Asin added, shaking her head.

"True. The second level seems to be the best level for the Farmers for now," Liev mused before he let his eyes wander over the stones again. "Anything else?"

"No, that's about it," Daniel said.

"Well, you're still in the lead," Liev reassured the group as he finished totaling up their earnings. "I'm sure you'll work out a plan to get through the floor soon."

"I think, well, it shouldn't be a problem tomorrow," Daniel replied, glancing to his friends, who offered nods in exchange. It seemed strange to be progressing through floors so quickly, but really, the first few floors had mostly been a matter of searching for the exits at their levels.

"Well, I guess we'll see you tomorrow," Daniel said, waving goodbye.

"Yes, tomorrow," Liev said as he worked to hide his yawn.

Outside, the group glanced at one another before Daniel spoke up, "Drinks at the Top?"

Quick nods of confirmation lead to the group taking a stroll down to the nearby inn. The Spinning Top was not the only inn in town, but it had three things that made it a popular watering hole. Firstly, the cooking was above average to superb. Secondly, Elise kept a clean and well-mannered location. And thirdly, and perhaps most importantly, it was close to the town center. For weary Adventurers, finding a place to sit and eat after a long day's delve ensured that the Top was constantly busy when the Dungeon was open.

Inside, Daniel quickly spotted and snagged the very last open table. It was in the far corner of the inn, a decent distance from the fireplace but also the farthest away from the Top's most recent star attraction—the Crimson Elms. Seated on their chairs, the group regaled the rapt audience with tales of an Advanced Dungeon.

Any other day, any other group, Daniel would have been right there with the rest of the Adventurers, drinking in the stories like the lifeblood they were. Stories, no matter how exaggerated, often held hints for Beginner Adventurers of what to expect in future Dungeons. A survivor, no matter the reason why, had something to teach. And in a profession where so many died, any crumb of knowledge was important.

"They cleared the third floor today," Elise said as she deposited the tankards of ale and a cup of sabu for Asin. The Catkin immediately grabbed her drink, sticking her nose in the rim and inhaling the sweet smell of fermented fruits.

"Oh?" Daniel tried to feign unconcern, which made Elise smile.

"Yes. They were telling that story earlier," Elise said. "Three of today's special?"

"Four!" roared Omrak as he lowered the tankard of ale and wiped at his mouth. "And another drink!"

"Right away." Elise smiled, heading back to the bar to pass on the order.

"I had to kill the Griffon Champion all alone while Rickard and Will were holding the rest off. Harald was out of Mana after calling his Gravity Well spell and grounding the Griffons. Now, I …"

"Ouch!" Daniel snapped as he pulled his arm back and rubbed at the spot where Asin's claw had drawn blood. He turned away from listening to the Crimson Elm's leader to focus on his own party.

"Talking," Asin said. "Tomorrow, we run?"

Daniel blinked and nodded, rubbing his chin. It was the continuation of the discussion while they waited.

"I say not. They are small monsters. Unworthy of running from," rumbled Omrak. "We should walk forward with confidence. We know how to defeat those Worms now."

"You know," Daniel grumbled. Unlike the rest of them, Omrak had the ability to stab his sword straight down into the ground due to his combined Skill Proficiencies. He could spear the monster as it rose, injuring and driving it away. It made him entirely safe from the attacks. "The rest of us are working it out."

"Bah. Your Skill injures them," Omrak said.

"If I hit at the right time. Too early and it does nothing."

"Is same for me," Omrak shrugged. "All fights are a risk."

"Run," Asin said. "Down. More monsters. Coin."

Daniel nodded to that. It was a definite point. The level seemed to be straightforward—all they had to do was run in a straight line along the path to find the exit. If they did that, they should find it. They might skip the Champion this round, but if they could complete the level, they might earn more on the next level. Pride or not, their goal was to earn coin after all. Today's earnings were even lower than yesterday's. In the end, it was his shrinking coin purse that made up Daniel's mind. "We'll run."

Omrak hmphed and crossed his arms. His sulk lasted until the plates of sliced lamb appeared, at which point it disappeared as quickly as the food into his mouth. Asin inhaled the strong scent of lamb mixed with herbs, doused in a gravy of fermented bean and meat juice. She grinned, slicing apart the potatoes first and dragging the tuber along the gravy before popping the meal into her mouth. She sighed slightly, the mixture of rich thick gravy and steamed potatoes settling her hunger.

Plans made, the group fell silent. Tomorrow would be interesting.

***

Jogging in full plate sucked, Daniel decided. It was hot, it was heavy, and it was exhausting. Ahead of him, he could see Asin crouched with a hand to the ground, feeling for the tremors that indicated a Worm. Daniel had left his crossbow behind, having decided against the extra weight today, so it would be up to Asin and Omrak to protect them against the birds. Not that Daniel himself had been of any real use before anyway.

Omrak, beside him, jogged along easily, chuckling at Daniel. Without armor, the giant barbarian had a much easier time of it. "There are more birds now than ever."

"Yes," Daniel panted.

"I believe they come because we have not stopped," Omrak rumbled, gesturing above. "I fear we run into danger."

Daniel nodded, waving to Asin to stay where she was. She frowned, raising an eyebrow in enquiry when they closed.

"We must fight soon. Or if we are forced to later, we will be at a disadvantage," said Omrak.

Asin growled and then looked up before curling her claws on the ground. "One closing. Maybe outrun. If Daniel faster."

"Not happening," Daniel gasped as he sucked in lungfuls of air. He forced himself not to bend over, to stay standing. He did, however, pull his helmet off to cool down and allow himself to drink from his waterskin easier.

"Fight."

"Good," rumbled Omrak as he stepped aside and unsheathed his sword before burying it in the ground and stripping off his shirt. Undressed, Omrak lifted his sword again and began to tap it on the ground, just lightly as he waited in an attempt to draw the monster to him. Daniel moved aside quickly to give Omrak space as he scanned the horizon.

"Is that the Elms?" Daniel said as he squinted back the way he came. In the distance he could see figures moving and the Elms were the only others on the fourth floor thus far. A moment later, he saw the birds that had collected above the other group suddenly collapse as if a giant hand had crushed them. The Elms broke apart and alternately stomped, kicked, stabbed, and smashed the ground. Or more likely, the monsters that were on the ground. It took the group barely a half-minute before they started walking again. "I guess that's what Gravity Well does …"

"Focus," Asin hissed at Daniel, and he found himself grimacing again. Right, they had their own monsters coming in soon. He fell silent, head bent as he focused on the trembling in the earth as the monster coasted inside the ground. Daniel was once again grateful that whatever made it possible for the Tremqua Worms to move at such speed underground also made it possible to detect them so easily.

Asin yowled slightly, arching her back in anticipation of jumping, before she looked to where Omrak continued to bang on the ground. Omrak stopped his tapping after a moment and then roared as he plunged the blade into the earth, leaping backwards immediately after.

Cued to attack, Daniel dashed towards the sunken blade. The Tremqua Worm burst forth from the ground, injured by the strike with its mouth torn open on one side. Even as it raised itself off the ground and twisted to hide again, Daniel reached it. The stocky Adventurer roared as he loosed Perin's Blow, smashing the monster higher into the air. The Worm's body elongated under the attack and pulped under the mace, splattering Daniel with warm blood.

Above, the birds dived and were met by Asin's Fan of Knives. The survivors flocked closer, the lead bird struck by Omrak's thrown axe and falling to the ground in a bloody fan of feathers and meat. Daniel paid no attention to what was going on above him as he pounded on the Tremqua Worm with his Skill. Even the bird that attempted to pierce his armor with its razor sharp beak and peck at his body from its perch on the ground failed to draw his attention.

Asin almost chuckled as she watched Daniel, one hand swinging and cutting any attacker while the other tossed knives underhand. The Catkin would have to spend a few minutes finding all of them later on, but it was why she marked each knife with her scent each morning. It was a tactic that only worked for a Beastkin and one she had not shared with her party members, nor did she intend to. Asin idly hopped to the side, scooping up another pair of knives she had left in the ground for easy access while they waited and continued her attack.

One last blow and Daniel rose fully, idly catching a swooping bird against his shield. The raptor smashed directly into it, its claws and wings compressing briefly before it found itself on the ground, stunned by the sudden stop. Daniel stepped forwards quickly, stomping down on an exposed wing as he surveyed the battlefield.

Omrak, bare-chested and bleeding again, was swinging his sword around and batting birds to the ground around him. Occasionally the Northerner would take a step aside as injured raptors attempted to hop their way to him. Injured and bleeding though he might be, Daniel could tell that Omrak was not being hindered by his injuries. Knowing that, Daniel took the time to attack the monsters that had been grounded. Omrak's fighting methods were strong, powerful, and dangerous—but they were not designed to allow a Healer to approach and lay hands on him for healing. It was a definite concern and one that had Daniel considering learning the ranged variations of his healing spells.

Minutes later, the group found themselves free of monsters. During the cleanup, a second Tremqua Worm had surfaced and attempted to attack Asin. The agile Catkin had proceeded to jump straight into the air and throw a Piercing Shot directly down its throat, immediately killing the monster, much to Daniel's chagrin. In truth, locating and picking up the various Mana Stones was more difficult than the initial fight.

"Better?" Daniel asked as he glanced at Omrak, who stood stretching, his wounds scabbed over and slowly healing under Daniel's spell.

"Yes. My thanks again, Hero Daniel. It is a marvelous thing to have a Healer in your party."

Asin chuffed her agreement before looking around the ground once more. Satisfied they had collected both knives and stones, she pointed down the road. Time to go. The Crimson Elms were on their way.

***

"I need a break," Daniel said, his breathing heaving hours later. The only reason it had taken so long before he called it quits again was his Healing magic, and even that was limited by the amount of Mana he dared use. "How big is this level?"

"Big," Asin said.

"It does seem extensive," Omrak added, shaking his head as he surveyed the land around him. Twice more already the group had needed to pause to deal with the building numbers. Behind them, the Crimson Elms continued to trudge onwards, more than content to let the Tremqua Worms attack as they walked. "It reminds me of stories of the Lowna Plains."

"It reminds me of the road from Peel," muttered Daniel wryly. Flat, boring and endless that road had been. "You know, this level might end up being an easy one for most groups."

"Hmmm?" Asin growled as she chewed on a strip of jerky.

"The monster attacks are few and far between. Once you know what to expect, it isn't difficult to deal with. It's also a single flat plain, so if there are a lot of parties, you might not even be attacked," Daniel explained. "In other levels, you don't want to cluster up. Too narrow corridors, too small caverns. Here, there's no reason not to."

Omrak nodded slightly, rubbing his chin. "Yes. And the features are the same as before. Unlike the second floor, where the water levels alter the paths."

"Exactly. No surprises, no changes. This will be an easy level," Daniel said, his breathing slowly coming under control. Pulling some jerky from his own pouch, he began to chew on it as he waved for the group to start walking. They would eat and move.

"Why?" Asin asked and waved her hand around the Dungeon at their puzzled glances.

Daniel shrugged and Omrak stayed silent. It was generally believed that Panqua, Erlis's, son was the one who managed the actual Dungeons. Apocryphal stories even had Adventurers running into the god in Dungeons, gifting reward and punishment for those who succeeded and failed spectacularly in equal measure. Still, stories from the church or not, no one actually understood why or how he did what he did or when. Because of that, most Adventurers ignored what little was known, focusing on the rather more important day-to-day aspects of surviving the Dungeons.

***

It was late afternoon by the time the Elms finally caught up with the group. As the day lengthened, Daniel found himself slowing down even further, such that the group had taken to just walking for the last few hours. That had increased the number of Worms who latched onto the group, which forced them to slow down further and wait for each attack.

"Not running anymore?" their leader said the moment they had caught up. Daniel pressed his lips together, refusing to rise to the bait, while Asin just growled.

"No," Omrak replied cheerily. "We see no end to this level as yet."

"Well, you did well. For a Beginner group," she continued. "If you follow close enough, we'll keep the monsters off your back too."

"It would be our honor to join in glorious battle with such great Heroes," Omrak said.

"That's not—"

"Ah, you would prefer not to fight such paltry monsters? We will be honored to ensure your weapons are not demeaned by their blood."

"No—"

"No need for thanks, great Hero," Omrak continued, waving his hands around. "We will do our best to fight under the eyes of ones so great. Perhaps some pointers would be helpful."

"Look, you—"

"Leave it, Amrah. We'll move faster if we aren't having to deal with the monsters," said the Mage.

Amrah looks dissatisfied at that, growling softly beneath her breath. Still, she said nothing further as she stomped onwards. The large warrior on their side followed quietly, though the slightest smile could be seen on his lips.

"Thank you, great Heroes!" Omrak called.

In answer, the Mage raised his hand and called forth his spell, the birds that had gathered falling to the earth. The Crimson Elms continued their walk while the trio found themselves dealing with the injured monsters. When they were done, the Elms had already moved on, leaving them to collect the Mana Stones.

"Did you do that on purpose?" Daniel said.

"Do what?" Omrak replied, a wide smile still on his face. Daniel squinted at the large barbarian suspiciously while Asin just snorted, continuing to pick up the Mana Stones.

"Hurry. Catch up," Asin said, pointing to the group a distance ahead.

"Right, right." This was going to be a long day.

Chapter 7

"A day and a half journey, eh?" Liev said, rubbing his chin. He stared at the tired, dusty trio that stood before him. "That explains the lack of monster attacks."

"Uhhh …" Daniel said.

"Levels require Mana to create. The larger the level, the more Mana. Beginner Dungeons are Beginner Dungeons partly because there is only so much Mana that they have access to. It's why they are limited to ten levels," Liev continued. "More Mana spent on a level to make it larger means less monsters."

"Interesting," Asin said approvingly.

"You did not fight the Champion?" Liev asked, glancing at the stones before him.

"No, the Elms did."

"Did you see it?"

"Yes. It was enormous—thrice as large as a normal Worm. No birds, though—not any more than normal," said Daniel. "Tough and you have to be much more careful than before. You really can get injured."

"Did you reach the fifth level?" Liev asked as he finished totting up their earnings.

"Yes. We didn't explore, though," Daniel said. "It was just a room with a door. Didn't want to test the door out."

"A door?" Liev said, running a hand through his red hair. "Well, might be many things. Going in tomorrow then?"

"Definitely," Daniel said. His earlier misgivings were still there, but after meeting the group, he knew he would not give up. If they lost, they lost—but he was not about to let the arrogant Crimson Elms saunter in without any challenge.

Asin beside him just nodded, already splitting the coins. The pile was significantly higher than their previous trip. Playing clean-up for the Elms had at least been highly profitable, if demeaning. She quietly handed the coins over to each group member before flashing the group a grin and offering a wave before she left.

Omrak picked up the coins, sliding them into his pouch. The barbarian stretched before he spoke. "I shall see you tomorrow. Hero Daniel. Attendant Halliope."

Daniel nodded goodbye, pocketing his own coin as he headed out.

In the inn, Daniel sighed, stripping a shirt off to wipe himself down. As frustrating as the day was, he did have one small thing to smile about.

Name: Daniel Chai

Class: Level 8 Adventurer (02%)

Sub-classes: Level 7 (Miner) (31%)

Human (Male)

Statistics

Life: 257

Stamina: 257

Mana: 186

Attributes

Strength: 25

Agility: 22

Constitution: 29

Intelligence: 19

Willpower: 19

Luck: 14

Skills

Unarmed Combat: Level 3 (43/100)

Clubs (Novice): Level 1 (14/100)

Archery: Level 2 (48/100)

Shield: Level 9 (74/100)
Dodge: Level 6 (23/100)
Combat Sense: Level 7 (18/100)
Perception: Level 7 (04/100)
Mining: Level 7 (78/100)
Healing: Level 9 (64/100)
Herb Lore: Level 3 (31/100)
Stealth: Level 2 (24/100)
Cooking: Level 3 (99/100)
Singing: Level 2 (14/100)

Skill Proficiencies
Double Strike
Shield Bash
Perin's Blow
Mapping (II)

Spells
Minor Healing (I)
Healer's Mark (I)

Gifts
Martyr's Touch—The caster may heal oneself or others by touch and concentration, sacrificing a portion of his life to do so. Cost varies depending on the extent of the injuries healed.

The increase to his attributes was as always, extremely helpful and been quickly allocated. Daniel also had a Skill Proficiency point to allocate this Level. He had a few options, including taking some of the Skills he had ignored or upgrading an existing Skill, but there was also new options to consider.

The first was from achieving a Novice level in Club Proficiency. He had two options at this point. He could either purchase **Mighty Blow,** which was a more powerful version of **Power Strike,** or he could purchase **Elemental Blow**. It imbued his own attacks with an additional elemental force, much like the elemental bracers that he once wore and that Asin still did.

In addition, with a higher Skill level in Combat Sense, he now had the option of purchasing a new Combat Sense-related Skill called **Find Weakness**. It was a Skill Proficiency that innately made him understand where he could attack to increase the amount of damage. This was particularly important when fighting new monsters, since their weak spots were not always apparent immediately.

As always, he could also dedicate his Skill Proficiency to increasing one of his existing Skills, but those, while useful were not particularly interesting. One day perhaps, he might acquire **Triple Strike**, but for now, it's beginner variation worked well enough. Nor did he desire to spend his point on upgrading his Healing spells. At the very least, he wanted to wait till he could acquire a ranged variation.

Both new options were powerful for different reasons, but in the end, he found himself selecting **Find Weakness**. The reason was simple. **Elemental Blow** required him to use Mana, something that he needed for Healing. **Find Weakness**, on the other hand, was a passive Skill Proficiency and thus was more powerful overall.

Having made his decision, he selected it and looked over the information silently.

Find Weakness

Increased understanding of opponents and ability to detect weaknesses.

Skill: Passive

Cost: N/A

Effect: User has a 20% + 5% chance per level of Combat Sense to find weakness

Satisfied with his choice, Daniel sighed and closed his eyes. Even if it was in the middle of the day, the Adventurer had been awake and moving for a day and a half as it stood. He was exhausted and tired and really just needed some rest.

***

Later that evening, Khy'ra pushed open the door to his room. She laughed, seeing the sprawled-out form of the Adventurer as he lay there, shirtless with a touch of drool slipping out of the corner of his mouth. The Elf moved into the room, pushing against Daniel's discarded clothing on his desk to clear some room for the food she had been acquired downstairs.

"Daniel," Khy'ra said as she gently pushed against his shoulder.

"Mmmrrpphfff."

"Daniel, dinner," Khy'ra said again, prodding his shoulder harder. He rolled over and the Elf grinned impishly, sneaking a finger between his armpits to tickle it.

"Aaargh!" Daniel said, sitting up and glaring at her.

"Evening," Khy'ra said, leaning over and kissing him on the lips. "I brought dinner. You need to eat."

"Mmm … I guess." Daniel rubbed at his face to clear the sleep from his eyes before he swiped at his mouth just before his stomach growled. "What would I do without you?"

Khy'ra fell silent at those words, turning away to pick up the plates and return with them to the bed. She handed Daniel's plate to him while she began to poke at the crust of her pie to mix it in.

"Did I say something?" Daniel asked, frowning at the sudden change of atmosphere.

"No, you didn't. Not really. It's just, well, you are going to be gone soon," Khy'ra said. "It's just coming up so fast."

"Oh …" Daniel blinked, shaking his head, and then he reached out and hugged her. "I'm sorry."

"It's fine," Khy'ra said, her voice soft and slightly tired. "It's fine. It's not as if I didn't know to expect this."

Daniel nodded into her hair, just hugging her harder. That too was true.

"Eat," Khy'ra said again, elbowing him slightly to make him let her go. "I keep telling you that recently don't I?"

Daniel laughed slightly, and then turned to his pie. She was right. Still … he would miss her. They ate in silence for a time, both of them lost in their own thoughts, before Khy'ra shook her head, visibly pushing the morose thoughts aside.

"Come. Summer is not ended," she said.

"It's autumn."

Khy'ra smiled, kissing him on the lips. "Now, tell me about your delve."

"Well, we tried running the floor. That was a mistake. If I didn't have my Gift …" Daniel said, Khy'ra leaning in with interest.

Chapter 8

Standing on the fifth floor after the first doorway, the group stared at the small tile-set arrayed before them and the locked door. Even Omrak's great strength had been unable to budge the handle and striking the door had not worked either. It was obvious that they were meant to solve the puzzle of the tiles.

"What do we do?" Daniel said, staring at the set of multi-colored tiles. It was a large set, thirty pieces wide and thirty pieces long with a series of five colors. All the spaces but one were filled.

"Move?" Asin growled, pointing at the tile space that was open.

"I guess," Daniel said, and glanced at Omrak, who shrugged.

"Right, move it is," Daniel said, and gently pushed one tile to the next. The moment he did, three of the red tiles that were now in a same line shimmered and disappeared. "Huh."

Omrak glanced down at the tile set, noting the disappearance before he returned his gaze back to the room, his sword held at the ready. Asin's lips peeled backwards in a predatory grin before she prodded another tile in the open space to make a set of four. These tiles shimmered and disappeared, other tiles above clanking together as if pulled by a force. This created another set of colored tiles which disappeared too before the experience repeated once more.

Without being asked or asking, Asin began to move the pieces. Daniel watched her for a few moments more, before he finally turned away to stare around the room. A few minutes later, Asin let out a frustrated yowl. The Catkin had seven pieces left and three colors, none of which could be shifted. Unable to continue, the board shimmered.

At the same time, a portion of the wall lowered, and a trio of elemental turtles waddled out. Immediately, Omrak jumped forwards and started attacking the creatures, his giant sword cutting and smashing the monsters. Daniel jerked himself to a stop, waiting for a monster to make its way pass Omrak before he could attack. Asin just waited, the room too small for her thrown weapons to come into play safely.

After the monsters were killed, Asin looked back to the board, which had reset itself with a different configuration of tiles. Lips pursed, she nodded to herself and started to move tiles around.

***

"Asin, can one of us have a try?" Daniel asked as he watched Omrak pick up the ex-Kobold's Mana Stone.

"No," Asin snarled, glaring at the board.

"Okay." Daniel backed off. After over a dozen rotations, Asin seemed to have gotten better, with only a few final tiles left. "The better you do, the easier the monsters that come out when you fail."

"I would almost ask you to fail more, Hero Asin," Omrak said, glancing around the walls. "The monsters we have fought have been less than challenging."

"No. Pass," Asin said as she prodded at the board. Daniel sighed, and he went back to leaning against the door. So far it seemed that every wall could open, so the doors themselves were the only stable portion of the room.

***

"JAKA!" Asin shouted, jumping to her feet and laughing.

"Finished?" Daniel asked as he pushed himself off the door. Asin nodded, proud, as Omrak walked to the door, his sword held ready. Asin jumped over to the door, grabbing at the handle and yanking it open. Inside, there was just another room.

"Oh hell," Daniel muttered as they all walked in. "This is a puzzle floor, isn't it?"

Asin nodded and the trio looked around the room, taking it in. There was a single mauve-colored door in the room with a small cylindrical tube that was attached to the door where a handle would be. In the center of the room were three containers filled with red-, blue-, and yellow-colored liquids and a separate, empty container.

"We must match the liquid colors to the door," Omrak said.

"You know of this?" Daniel said.

"It is a common puzzle," Omrak said as he walked forwards. "May I?"

"Sure ..." Daniel said.

Asin blinked as the large Northerner began to pour the colored waters into the empty container without hesitation. It took barely a few seconds before Omrak was done, holding the container up to the light.

"Good?" Asin asked, peering at the container and its contents. An unfortunate aspect of being a Catkin was her reduced ability to judge colors, at least as the humans saw it.

"A touch more red," Omrak said, and walked back, fixing the liquid quickly before he poured the entire concoction into the handle. The door shuddered for a moment and Daniel hefted his mace, wary of additional monsters. He only relaxed when the door popped open and another empty room was showcased.

"Good." Asin loped forwards, clapping Omrak on the shoulder. Omrak just shrugged, accepting the compliment.

***

"Did we just get transported back to the start?" Daniel asked, staring around. The last puzzle they had faced was a riddle. A single wrong answer and they were back in the tile room. Daniel exhaled roughly as he stared at the tile set Asin had taken charge of once more.

"It does appear so, Hero," Omrak said.

"Daniel. It's Daniel," Daniel muttered irritably as he rested against the door again.

"Of course, Hero Daniel."

"No. Just Daniel."

"Yes, Hero Just Daniel."

"You're joking, right?"

Omrak just smiled while he glanced back to Asin and the tile set to see how far she had gotten.

After a second failed attempt by Asin, Daniel turned to Omrak. "What made you come to Karlak? There must have been closer Beginner Dungeons."

"Four," Omrak said. "None were suitable for melee fighters alone. I had planned to complete Karlak by myself."

"What changed?"

"Coin," Omrak answered with a self-deprecating laugh. "I could not progress as fast as I earned. A group aided that."

"Huh," Daniel said. The grinding of a wall rising made the stout Adventurer turn, glaring at the Kobold that came out. Idly, he caught the attack high on his shield and twirled his mace around, slamming it into the space between the

Kobold's third and fourth ribs, pulping its heart and killing it immediately.

"Asin, how are we doing?"

"Close. Easier now," she muttered, staring at the option she had now. Daniel just bent down to collect the Mana Stone before resting against the wall again. This was going to be another long day.

***

"Late day," Liev murmured, staring at the small portion of coins the trio offered.

"Puzzle floor," Daniel grumbled. At Liev's raised eyebrow, he detailed the floor for Liev who nodded.

"Ah, those were always enjoyable," Liev said, smiling at his own memories.

"Huh. For you maybe," muttered Daniel. Four times more the three had managed to get past the first room. They had even finished the third room once, but each failed attempt after the first room sent them back to the first room to start again. It did not help that the questions in the third room, like all the other puzzles, changed constantly, such that a correct answer once was no guarantee of a correct answer the next time.

Each new room was a different puzzle, the fourth a series of levers and ropes which controlled weights that had to be perfectly aligned. This puzzle Daniel had taken a shot at, and failed. Omrak continued to be the star performer of the group, never once failing to match the door's color.

"Are the Elms out yet?" Daniel asked.

"No," Liev said, shaking his head. He paused, staring at the trio before he continued slowly, "They might decide to spend a little time on this floor on purpose."

"Why?"

"They have a Mage with them," Liev said, as if that explained everything. The confused looks he gets from the others makes him continue. "Mages gain experience from knowledge and puzzle-solving. A puzzle floor like this could progress a novice Mage by a few levels."

"Oh …" Daniel said. Well, that made sense. Healers, real Healers with the Class and all, gained experience from Healing. It made sense that Mages would gain experience from puzzles and gathering knowledge.

"Best not to rush," Liev cautioned. "We lost Ilona's group today. Pierson's group found their corpses on the third floor next to the Champion."

"But … they were—" Daniel said, stuttering a little.

"Stronger than that? Not if you push too hard. A mistake and you're dead. You know that," Liev said, shaking his head. "Just because it's the lower level, it doesn't mean you can push it too hard."

Daniel grimaced as he accepted the coins from Asin. Liev was right, even if Daniel hated that fact. Caution, no matter what rewards were available, was important. They needed to slowdown and take it more cautiously, even if the fifth floor did not pay well. Even if they were not gaining much in terms of experience.

"Take care, Liev," Daniel said, waving goodbye to the red-haired attendant. Already, the others in his party had broken off, heading home after taking their share of the day's earnings. They had an early start tomorrow.

Chapter 9

"We should be exploring level seven, not playing stupid puzzles," snapped Amrah, as she stared at the Mage over dinner a week later in the Top. Daniel and Asin were quietly eating their meal not far from them that evening, enjoying the warmth from the fireplace close to them. The trio of Adventurers were still stuck on the fifth level, though at least they now knew that there were eight rooms in total. The last room held no puzzle, just the Floor Champion. If they could puzzle-out and beat the seventh room by tomorrow, they might finally be able to move on.

"We agreed to split our time," Harald the Mage said calmly. "Is this a formal request to change our agreement?"

Amrah growled but sat down with a thump, refusing to meet the Mage's eyes. A slight smile crossed Harald's face before he turned back to his drink. It had been over a week since their arrival and by now, the lure of an Advanced party had died down. There were still those who asked for and listened to the stories Amrah was more than willing to tell, but for the most part, the Adventurers had their own stories to tell.

The town buzzed with commerce now, and even Elise was talking of expanding her inn. The new levels had sparked the imagination of many wannabe-Adventurers who were arriving in a constant flow and taking up all the rooms in the inns throughout towns. Even experienced Beginners were willing to test out the new Dungeon, especially as the wider range of floors provided a more diverse training experience. Karlak was fast becoming a city that catered to a wide variety of Adventurers. It was said that Vinnie, the only bowyer in town, was now so busy that he had tripled his prices.

Daniel glanced at Asin, curious to see if she had noted the conversation. The Catkin offered a simple nod while she sipped on her Sabu, ears twitching a moment before she turned to the door with a smile. Khy'ra entered a moment later dragging along a protesting red-haired attendant. Spotting the two, she bee-lined towards them immediately.

"Daniel, Asin," Khy'ra greeted them before bending down to place a kiss on Daniel's lips. "Keep an eye on this one. And you. Sit."

Liev, grumbling, sat next to the bemused pair.

"I'm here under protest."

"Healer's orders," Khy'ra said as she plunked down a pair of foaming beer mugs. "Scoot. You're not dating Daniel."

Liev grunted, shifting seats and letting the Elf sit next to the stout Adventurer.

"Where's Omrak?"

"Dock," Asin said.

"He's still working down there?" Daniel asked, blinking. That he did not know. For that matter, how did Asin?

"Coin."

Khy'ra smiled slightly, listening to the pair, while Liev sucked down his beer.

"Not seen you out in a while, Liev." Daniel turned to the redhead. Liev coughed, clearing his throat as he finished up his beer.

"Yes. Well, a new Dungeon requires a significant amount of work. A very large amount of work," Liev said, and sighed. "I really should be back there. There are reports to file, maps to be commissioned, complaints to deal with …

"Owww!"

"No. You need a night out. And some decent food," Khy'ra said, pulling her hand back.

"You didn't have to hit me," Liev muttered, rubbing the top of his head.

"No, but it was fun," Khy'ra mocked the old attendant before she shook her head. "Gods, this reminds me of the last time I had to drag you for a break."

"In Corabia?" Liev said.

"Yes," Khy'ra said, smiling slightly. "We had to pull you from the library by force just to get you to eat after three weeks."

"They had dozens of books I never did see anywhere else. I had to copy them down," Liev said.

"That's what you always said." Khy'ra rolled her eyes.

"You two adventured together?" Daniel asked, glancing at the pair.

"Yes. It's good to get out once in a while and keep the hand in," Khy'ra said, smiling. "Not that we do it much these days, but …"

"But bills must be paid," Liev finished for her. "And we've all got expensive habits."

"The Clinic isn't a habit." Khy'ra pouted and Daniel nodded, giving her a quick squeeze around her waist. The waitress walked by, dropping off their plates.

"Of course not," Liev replied, smiling quietly as he scooped up some mashed potatoes on his fork. He paused, holding the fork in hand, and added musingly, "We never did make it to the Rysy Spires."

"No. Maybe another time," Khy'ra replied.

"Isn't that the Master Dungeon?" Daniel said. "One of a dozen in the world?"

"Yes. One of the two that lie within the borders of Brad," Liev said. It was actually part of the reason why the Kingdom had as much sway as it did. As Adventurers made up a significant portion of the Kingdom's armed forces, their ability to conveniently progress within the confines of the Kingdom ensured that they could contribute significantly to any conflict. It also meant that they often would act as ambassadors when they visited nearby kingdoms to clear those Dungeons.

"Dechen Cave?" Asin said, pointing between the two.

"Not me," Liev answered, shaking his head. "Nothing interesting there for a Mage. No spell books or tomes or anything else."

"Just a couple of times," Khy'ra answered.

"Couple?" Asin's eyes widened, staring at the Elf.

"I was led through it the first few times," Khy'ra reassured Asin, waving a hand down. "It's not as difficult as most think."

Liev snorted at her mock humility. Daniel just sat there, staring at his girlfriend. There obviously were a few things that he did not know about the beautiful Elf. Or, considering how old she was—probably more than a few things.

Still, he leaned over and murmured into her ear, "Is that how you keep the Clinic funded?"

"Mostly. I get donations of course and they help," she replied in a whisper, glancing over at Liev. "I hope you don't mind. He just needs some time away, but he won't take it."

"No," Daniel chuckled and then suddenly grinned. "Liev, so you've delved with Khy'ra before. I'm sure you've got a few stories …"

Khy'ra let out a little gasp and proceeded to glare at Daniel. He chuckled at his girlfriend's reaction until she elbowed him in the ribs, whereupon he gave her a quick kiss before looking back to his new prey. The red-haired attendant watched the byplay between the two before he smiled, saying, "Well … there are a few. There was this time in Sopot …"

Daniel settled in with Asin to listen to Liev talk of Khy'ra and their old adventures. Yet, in the corner of his mind, he turned over the idea of the two Master Dungeons, one of which even his accomplished girlfriend had not completed.

Chapter 10

"Is it just me or is this Dungeon a lot weirder than it used to be?" Daniel asked the next day, his eyes wide. It only took them a single try to make it all the way through the other rooms and now they stared at their last obstacle—the Floor Champion. The Champion's room itself was bare bones, illuminated by a series of torches with flames of varying colors.

"Weirder," Asin confirmed.

"What do we attack?" Omrak said, his voice puzzled.

"Ummm …" Daniel squinted at the monster, which was made of colored squares that constantly shifted. The monster had no head or true body, the entirety of its form morphing and twisting. Stranger, the colors in each block shifted as well. Daniel's new Skill Proficiency did not seem to be giving him any hints as yet as the monster lacked any eyes, ears or other clear weaknesses. "Hit them all and see what happens?"

"Fan?" Asin asked, pulling a series of knives from her hand.

"That works. Omrak and I will follow up if we see anything. Omrak, go high and I'll go low," Daniel decided firmly as he leaned back around the doorway and cranked his crossbow to insert a bolt.

"Ready," Daniel said.

Asin flicked a glance to Omrak who gave a single nod before she spun around the corner and dashed into the room, throwing her knives and triggering her Skill Proficiency. Her knives bloomed, multiplying and striking the monster across its cubed bodies. Most deflected off the creature's armor, only a pair sinking into a blue cube.

Immediately, Daniel sighted and fired his arrow at a blue cube that was holding the creature off the ground. Omrak cast his throwing axe as well, but both attacks bounced off. Daniel hesitated, confused for a moment at this unexpected development. A moment and then he released his crossbow, allowing it to drop to the ground as he charged the monster.

Omrak was ahead of him, swinging his sword at each cube while dodging the sudden changes in direction as best he could. Asin scampered to the side as well, flinging her knives at random cubes as they attempted to figure out what the puzzle solution in this case was.

"Green!" Ormak roared as his blade sank into the colored cube. He tore the blade out even as Daniel, a moment later managed to land his own successful blow. Asin's thrown knife a few seconds later clattered off a similarly colored cube at the creature's top.

Omrak, his attacks no longer working, had switched to randomly striking again. A sudden shift in the cubic body resulted in the Northerner being smashed without warning, throwing him back. Daniel, nearby, could almost swear he heard the bones break. He had no time to pay attention to his friend as the monster now turned its attention to him. Forced to defend himself, Daniel worked his shield and mace together to block and parry attacks that came in sudden surges of colored blocks.

Omrak returned to the battle in a violent explosion, his sword bashing the monster away from Daniel. Daniel exhaled with relief, spending a moment to catch his breath. There had to be a pattern to how you could win, but so far, they had not figured it out. The vulnerable cubes did not change after each attack, nor did they rotate in any specific order or location. They were timed in some way but that in itself was not sufficient. Daniel drew another deep breath, readying himself to step forwards, when the light flickered again. Drawn to the torches, he frowned. One torch, the one that was colored green, seemed stronger than the others right now.

Acting on instinct, he called out the color. Asin did not break step as she avoided an attack and sank a knife into an exposed green cube. Omrak was too busy to attack as he defended himself and by the time Daniel ducked and twisted out of the way from the monster's attacks, the flame had flickered. However, Daniel could see Asin's blade embedded in the green cube.

"Yellow," Daniel called out as he slammed his mace into the appropriately colored cube. "The torches. Follow the torches!"

Once they had figured out the monster's vulnerability, the battle became easier. Each attack that injured the monster slowed it down further, made the shifting in blocks jerkier. Attacks that had bruised and injured before were made simple to avoid or block, and when the monster finally stopped rotating and twisting, the trio collapsed, tired. Daniel groaned slightly as he forced himself up, walking over to Omrak to cast Healer's Mark on him and then moving to Asin, who was rubbing at her ankle. He smiled slightly at her nod before he pulled open the Floor Chest to pocket the Mana Stone. Well, that was not so bad. Certainly, the information would be something that Liev would be grateful for.

***

As the group entered the sixth floor, they were forcefully reminded of the previous second sector of the Dungeon, where the Draxillan Crawler used to live. Unlike the previous caves, the passages here were all on one level. but they were very much caves with dirt floors, dripping waters, and passages that they had to walk through.

"Crawlers?" Daniel muttered, looking around. This seemed similar, but the fact that it was all on one level seemed to indicate another type of monster was here. Perhaps the Dungeon just decided to repeat the similar layout because it was easier. Or was it the god, Panqua? Was he influenced by what had been present before? Did Dungeons or Panqua care?

"No." Omrak walked forwards and pointed to the ground. "These tracks are different."

Asin walked over, squatting down and running clawed fingers along the tracks. She held her palm out to them, measuring size and later, depth with furrowed brows. Humanoid tracks, in a way. "Thin."

"Yes, definitely," Omrak said. "Skeletons?"

Asin hissed at the mention before she stood and pulled out her melee knife. Daniel hefted his own mace as he stepped forwards to take the lead on instinct. Omrak growled softly as he stared at the corridors before he sheathed his own sword and pulled out a throwing axe to wield.

"Well, let's try this out," Daniel muttered, walking forwards into the dark, lit only by the torch that Omrak helpfully held for them. After all, they had time since they had completed the previous floor so quickly. At the least, they could learn what monsters they were to face.

A part of Daniel sighed, wondering if he would ever get to use his crossbow. It certainly felt like he kept getting relegated to being the melee fighter—even Omrak was better and faster with his throwing axes than he was. Then again, perhaps if he spent more time on the range, it would help as well.

Daniel's musings about his shortcomings came to an abrupt end as the clinking, grating sound of bone knocking on bone travelled through the air. He frowned as he raised his shield higher before entering the cavern. Inside he quickly spotted a dozen skeletons, held together by eldritch means. Bones floated above one another or scraped together when a movement came too fast like when the creatures turned to the new intruder, mouths opened wide. To Daniel's surprise, the group let loose an unnerving, otherworldly howl that froze the Adventurers in their tracks while the Skeletons charged.

As the first Skeleton reached him, swinging its boney hands at Daniel's face, Daniel jerked back, brought to his senses by the attack. His helmet saved his eyes and face, but the monster still left a long, bleeding scratch against his exposed chin. The pain shocked Daniel into action, his mace swinging sideways to beat a hand aside even as he hunkered down beneath his shield.

Behind, Asin was shocked awake by the underworld stench. Dry earth, musty bones, and something else, something unnatural, assaulted her sensitive nostrils. She snarled in a low rumble as she darted past the still-frozen Omrak, elbowing him in the side as she moved to guard Daniel's left.

Omrak grunted in shock, the pain bringing him back to the unfolding battle. Roaring in rage, Omrak stepped forwards to Daniel's side before he chopped down with his axe at an exposed bone. The shorter axe swung down, barely missing the stalactites that hung from the ceiling, before cracking into the collarbone of the skeleton. Again and again Omrak attacked, rage taking over his senses at the unnatural fear the monsters engendered within him. By sheer strength, Omrak was able to smash the bones apart, but it took multiple strikes.

Daniel with his mace was the most suited to this, the metal edges crushing and pulping bones with each strike. Occasionally, Daniel would take a step forwards and lash out against another monster to help the monsters focus on him as the spearhead of their tight triangle. Without weapons, the monsters were unable to injure the well-protected Adventurer, allowing him to wade into the group.

As Daniel pulled back from crushing the ribcage of one Skeleton, he found his mace arm grabbed. The Adventurer jerked backwards as he attempted to pull away but was unable to loosen the monster's grip. He struggled for a moment as the Skeleton threw its body on top of his arm, forcing Daniel to lift the entire monster. Another Skeleton grabbed at his shield as he was distracted, pulling it down as a third monster launched itself at the Adventurer directly. Only a last-minute lowering of his helmeted head allowed Daniel to protect his face as the monster tried to bite at the exposed flesh. Even still, the monster managed to sink its teeth into his cheekbone, ripping the flesh free.

Asin hissed, seeing Daniel trapped and fighting the monsters, but was unable to move to help. Each cut with her knife sent arcs of lightning along the opponents' yellowish-white bones, but the attacks seemed to do little. She could only buy time, distracting the monster as she attacked it, keeping it from piling on her friend.

Help came in the form of strong fingers as Omrak reached between the ribcage of the Skeleton holding Daniel's mace down, gripping the spine and lifting the monster upwards before tossing it at Omrak's former opponent. The action freed Daniel's arm at the cost of his mace. Able to move again, Daniel spun and smashed his gauntleted fist into the skull of the Skeleton that had latched itself on to his body in its attempt to eat his face. Daniel snarled and punched the monster again and again by instinct, fear, and anger mixed in equal measure as he pummeled his attacker.

When the Skeleton's head finally shattered apart, the bloody jawbone and skull falling to pieces, the creature dropped from Daniel's body. Panic subsiding slightly, Daniel stared at the Skeleton that still clutched at his shield, and triggered Shield Bash, slamming the shield a few inches forwards and throwing the Skeleton away.

"Here!" Omrak growled, tossing Daniel back his mace.

His weapon returned, Daniel stalked forwards to finish his own opponent. It took a brief few seconds for Daniel to smash apart his single enemy before he returned to give aid to

Asin, whose opponent was chipped but still standing.

"Looks like they die if you smash the skull open," Daniel said after he cast Healer's Mark on himself to begin the healing process.

"Yes. But it must be smashed fully," Omrak said, glaring around at the fading bones. Asin pulled her knife to her, testing the edge and grimacing.

"Knife no work," Asin complained, her tail wagging side to side.

"Aye, it is only my Skill that allowed me to use my axe," Omrak agreed. "And I am unable to use my sword in these caves."

"Back?" Asin asked, frowning as her tail lashed out behind her.

"I'm doing okay," Daniel pointed out. "Mostly."

"Do you believe we can complete the level with you leading the way?"

"Probably?" Daniel said, surveying the damaged skeletons that lined the floor. "This is only Level Six."

Omrak glanced at Asin, who just nodded resignedly. For a moment more, Omrak hesitated before he finally agreed. "Very well, Hero Daniel. We shall be in your hands."

"Then let's go. At the least, we can map out some of this level." Hefting his weapon, Daniel strode forwards.

***

It barely took them another twenty minutes before they found another group of Skeletons. Daniel approached quickly, rushing forwards and to the right as he bashed one monster into the other seven, leaving one untouched. The attacked Skeleton flew backwards, its lighter body no match for the greater strength and Skill. It slammed into the other monsters behind it, tangling the group up and causing a few to fall. Roaring in approval, Omrak dropped his axe to sweep his sword out of its sheath. This cavern was taller and wider, large enough that he could wield his weapon with ease. As the undead monsters struggled to their bony feet, Omrak laid into them with a vengeance. Asin in the meantime backed up Daniel, ready to step in to help him if he needed it.

Not that he did at this point. The single standing Skeleton reached outwards, attacking Daniel, but was blocked with a hard parry that cracked its arm bones. On the return, Daniel crushed its temple, sending the monster staggering backwards. Out of the corner of his eye, he saw that Omrak was about to be swarmed.

"Yours," Daniel shouted as he bull-rushed a Skeleton on the edges. This monster had lost its arm but showed no sign of slowing down as it attacked the Northerner. So intent was it on its objective, the Skeleton never saw Daniel's tackle that sent it flying into a nearby wall. Spinning on his feet, Daniel used the edge of his shield to crack the spine of another Skeleton before crushing its head with his mace.

Omrak, bleeding and beleaguered, was forced back further towards their entrance. The Skeletons continued their single-minded pursuit, leaving Daniel their exposed backs to attack. Seizing the opportunity presented to him, Daniel attacked with wide, powerful swings and quickly ended the fight. By the time he was done, Asin had finished chipping away at her own opponent.

"Easier," Asin growled.

"No scream," Daniel replied, and blinked. Ugh, he sometimes fell into Asin's talking pattern without thinking.

"Yes. Did we surprise them?" Omrak asked.

"Perhaps," Asin sniffed, and shrugged as she spent the time looking around for Mana Stones. Daniel bent down to help her, his eyes roaming over the two entrances. Left, or right? Truly, it did not matter right now—they just needed to map the Dungeon till they found the staircase down.

***

"This is going to take a while," Daniel said, shaking his head as he stared at the map only he could see. The minimap showed the sprawling complex they had walked in the last hours, multiple passageways that led from each cavern that had to be explored individually. Worse, they often found small passages which had to be carefully squeezed through and verified, as some of those passages would open into wider or larger caverns. It meant that they had moved slowly, checking side passages and small openings as they walked along. Eyeballing the map, Daniel sighed.

They had barely covered a quarter of the ground that a 'normal' level would have, and it was time to head back.

So busy was he that Daniel missed the small opening by his feet, his steps carrying him past before he could see the Skeleton that pushed itself free. Asin, who was directly behind Daniel and checking for traps ahead of them saw the monster too late. A boney hand grabbed her ankle, pulling her to her knees even as the Skeleton continued to crawl out of the hole, levering itself up along her body. Nails clawed into the Catkin, digging into fur and the flesh beneath, opening long wounds along her frame. Close enough now, the Skeleton bit down on an exposed thigh, teeth rending flesh.

As the Skeleton raised its head from the injury, blood running down its teeth, Omrak reached forwards and gripped the monster by its neck. Eschewing his axe, Omrak smashes the monster directly into the cave walls again and again. Skin and fur tore from Asin as the creature was ripped away, freeing the Catkin to send a Piercing Shot down the hole to crack the skull of the next Skeleton that pulled itself forwards.

Having heard the commotion behind him, Daniel turned around and quickly moved to take station before the hole.

"Sorry!"

Asin just yowled in frustration and pain as she backed away to let the warriors deal with this next threat as she scrambled for bandages. Forced to crawl out one by one, it was a simple matter for Daniel to end them all. Monsters torn apart, Daniel moved to place a hand on Asin, healing her as he muttered an apology again. This Dungeon wore one down, never letting you spend a single moment to yourself. Always, always there was a danger.

Asin, fur and skin slowly regrowing, bent down to pick up the Mana Stones and yowled unhappily, her tail lashing out behind her. So many were in her pouch now, but each Mana Stone dropped was tiny and dark, lacking none of the luster a good stone might have.

"Sorry again," Daniel said, looking around at last. "I missed it. Should have paid more attention. It was just so small."

"Small," Asin agreed.

"Har! You say so," Omrak grumbled, rubbing at his head where he accidentally knocked it again on a stalactite. The cavern in this portion of the Dungeon was so low that Omrak had knocked his head more than once. Already, Daniel had been forced to deal with one nasty bleeding scalp wound and an incipient concussion. "I fear this cave will end me before our opponents.".

"Good time to stop anyway. About time to go back," Daniel said, pointing back the way they came. "We won't finish this level today. Maybe not for a few days."

Asin nodded, scratching at an ear. "Map?"

"I'm making it," Daniel said.

"Buy," Asin said, shaking her head. "Elm sell?"

"Oh …" Daniel frowned but finally nodded. The Catkin was right, if there was a faster option here, they should go with it. Though he doubted the Elms were that confident that they would sell the location and route to the next stairway down.

He pondered that thought while he led the way back, their return uneventful but for a few further attacks, which the group dealt with simply enough. Still, by the time the party finally made their way into the Adventurers' Guild, the group was dragging their feet. It had been a long, cramped, and tiring day.

"Sixth floor?" Liev said, glancing at the crystals arrayed before him as he did the calculations. There were a lot certainly. "I hear it's infested with Skeletons."

"Infested. That works," Daniel said. "The Elms didn't sell a map, did they?"

Liev shook his head, swinging his pad around for Asin and Omrak to confirm before he drew forth the requisite cash.

"Didn't think so." Daniel sighed. This was definitely going to take a while.

Chapter 11

"How's it going?" Khy'ra asked Daniel as she lay in bed, watching the young man working at his desk. Daniel blinked and looked up from the parchment upon which he was drawing the map for the sixth floor. The party had spent four days on that level and it seemed that while it was not significantly larger than a 'normal' floor, the numerous connected and dead-end passages meant that more space was compacted into the same area. At least it did not seem like the level's layout changed.

"Slow. We might have to do an overnighter tomorrow if we want to finish it," Daniel said. "We keep running out of time."

Khy'ra smiled slightly, watching Daniel, before she stood up and walked over to look at his map. Blonde hair cascaded down her back as she did so, and Daniel took a moment to enjoy the view. The Elf smiled slightly when she noted that, leaning over to tap him on the nose while she glanced at the map. After a moment, her finger dropped to a blank spot on it.

"There. Your staircase will likely be around there."

"How do you know?"

"Experience," Khy'ra said before she held up a finger. She walked quickly over to her chest, bending low to wave a hand at it before she pulled forth a rolled-up map. Returning, she waved her hand over the map and murmured a word. Suddenly, lines began to trace over the map, quicker and quicker till before them was a detailed drawing of a Dungeon.

"Look familiar?" Khy'ra asked, and Daniel nodded. That was the third floor of the old Karlak Dungeon. The moment he did, Khy'ra said another word in Elvish and the map changed again.

"Peel, sixth floor."

"Porthos, seventh floor."

"Alytus, fifth floor."

"See the pattern?" Khy'ra asked after flipping through numerous Dungeon maps on her magical map.

"No …" Daniel said, shaking his head. If there was one, it was more subtle than he could see.

"Well, when you can, you'll start to understand how the Dungeon is laid out. Might save you some time in the future," Khy'ra said, and then glanced at his original map as she rolled up her own. "Of course, it won't help much with your problem."

"No, too many passages," Daniel confirmed, sighing.

"Come on, let's go to bed," Khy'ra said, tugging on his hand and laying an inviting kiss on his lips. "The Dungeon will still be there tomorrow."

Drawn by Khy'ra's hand, Daniel discarded the map behind him.

***

The next morning, Daniel was yawning as Asin walked up to the Dungeon entrance. She raised an eyebrow, surprised at seeing Daniel there before her.

"Early."

"Yes." Daniel yawned again, then smiled slightly. He reached down and picked up some brown packages wrapped in parchment paper and twine. "Don't have much of a lunch today. I did pick up some pack meals from the Guild for today and tomorrow."

Asin sniffed, obviously displeased, but took the packages to slip into her bag. As the wind shifted, she caught Daniel's scent and Khy'ra intermingled with their night's strenuous activities. Nose wrinkling, she stepped away to crouch beside the entrance.

"How are things going?" Daniel asked after a while to fill the silence.

"Good."

"Really? You've been pretty stressed about our earnings recently."

"Low," Asin agreed.

"Never seen you that worried before."

Asin just shrugged, not meeting his gaze.

"Asin, we're friends. You know you can talk to me about things, right?" Daniel probed again.

Again, the Catkin just nodded, and Daniel gave up, lips compressed in a tight line. Perhaps he would ask Khy'ra later when he had a moment. The two had certainly developed a curious relationship. Daniel's thoughts were interrupted as Omrak neared them. Daniel absently noted that Omrak was wearing a simple, visorless helm today, his first real piece of armor. Time to get to work.

***

"Ouch," Omrak growled, rotating his shoulder. A trio of Skeletons had managed to get hold of his hands, hampering his movements while a fourth had pounded on him. The group had found a cavern filled with Skeletons, their presence hidden by a convenient wall, and found themselves swarmed before they could pull back. Every single one of the party now bore wounds from the battle, Asin barely escaping with her life by scampering up a wall and staying out of reach of the Skeletons.

"Sorry. Nearly done," Daniel said. His plates of iron armor had protected him from most direct attacks, but between the gaps and along the edges where armor met cloth, he was scratched and bruised.

"No like," Asin said as she collected another stone and dropped it into her pouch. "Can't hurt."

Not exactly true, Daniel thought as he spotted a throwing knife and handed it back to his friend. Her Piercing Shot could drill through skulls, killing the monster immediately. Unfortunately, each use of her Skill drained her

Stamina, ensuring that she could only activate it occasionally. Otherwise, her attacks were minimally effective.

"Well, we've begun the unexplored region of this side of the map. Hopefully we'll find the way down soon," Daniel said placatingly. Not much else he could say. "When everyone's ready, that is."

"A minute," Omrak said, testing his shoulder again. It still pulled sharply when he rotated his shoulder, drawing a wince from the large blond man. "Perhaps I could use a Healer's Mark."

***

Hours of walking, squeezing, crawling, and occasionally climbing later, the party had mapped out another section of the Dungeon. Unfortunately, their last section had led to a dead-end, and so the group found themselves backtracking to their last unexplored location.

"That's ... new," Daniel muttered as he poked his head around the corner. Asin's warning had pulled the group to a halt before they entered, and now the trio watched the group of Skeletons and Skeleton Champion standing eerily still in a previously empty cave. The Skeleton Champion looked no different from its brethren except for a deeper, darker discoloration of its bones, and the pair of short swords it wielded.

"Champion," Asin growled softly, testing the edge of her throwing knife.

"See if we can kill it beforehand?" Daniel suggested.

"I can try," Omrak offered, hefting his throwing axe.

"Both."

On a silent count of three, the pair surged forth from their hiding spot and threw their respective weapons. The knife and throwing axe whipped through the air before they were deflected in quick succession by the Champion's swords.

Omrak stood there, stupefied, while Asin scrambled to pull her bolas from her belt. At least those worked, especially in such a large crowd. Daniel, seeing that the attack was finished, stepped forwards to take the charge.

The normal Skeletons rushed forwards, bones clicking together as they came on with their hands outstretched. The Champion stood still, however, instead issuing its paralyzing scream. The group winced as one, feeling the supernatural fear course through their limbs to slow them down. At least now, they had gained sufficient experience to resist the initial freezing effects of the scream. Even so, Asin found herself fumbling the grip of her bolas, dropping it on the earthen floor.

The first Skeleton was on Daniel before he could activate his Shield Bash, slowed down by the scream as he was. He could only hunker beneath the shield, taking the attack and stepping backwards to absorb the charge as even more Skeletons piled on. Seeing an opening, he roared and sent his Skill Perin's Blow directly into the ribcage of one monster, shattering the bones and sending them flying backwards in a hail of shards. Gravely injured, the monster collapsed at his feet, while Daniel stepped to the side to avoid a grasping arm.

Behind him, Omrak brought the pommel of his axe down on the crown of a Skeleton, compressing the monster and knocking it off its feet. With a backhand strike, he cleaved open the ribcage of another that was attempting to circle the group. This attack was minimally effective at deterring the creature as it regained its feet and continued its approach.

Finally on her feet again, Asin skipped backwards and to the left before tossing the bolas underhanded at a Skeleton in the back. It wrapped around the targeted monsters and another's legs, tangling both up and buying time for Daniel.

Using the brief moment afforded him, Daniel focused and let loose a Shield Bash against his current opponent, sending the monster stumbling backwards. In the opening, he engaged his Double Strike to crack a hip and then the skull of another Skeleton. Before he could reset his guard, a sword darted forwards, skipping along his chestplate and missing his face by inches. Not giving Daniel time to rest, the Skeleton Champion lashed out again with its other sword, a blow that was barely blocked by Daniel's shield.

The pair dueled for a moment, Daniel blocking attacks with his shield and mace, and the Champion cutting and stabbing with speed and precision. Daniel grunted as he stepped backwards again as he attempted to regain control of the fight. Unable to assist or hold the attention of the other monsters, the Skeletons began to circle around the Champion and Daniel to attack his friends.

Asin yowled as she scrambled backwards, throwing another bolo to entangle the feet of a Skeleton that chased her. It was a delaying tactic, but at least it meant she only had two to deal with. Beside her, Omrak roared as a Skeleton gripped his thigh, its mouth clamped around his leg. The Northerner was unable to deal with it as he held a second clawing Skeleton aloft by its ribcage and struck at a third even as another pair attempted to close in on him.

Daniel grunted as another strike slipped past his guard and bounced off his upper arm armor. The Skeleton Champion was significantly more skilled than he was, Daniel was quickly realizing. A muted cry of pain from behind him reminded him that Asin was in trouble and he made a quick decision, raising his shield slightly higher.

The Champion was quick to take advantage of the situation, its sword lashing out. Trusting in his armor, Daniel surged forwards at the same time, twisting his shield so that he could slam its edge into the Champion's neck even as he engaged Perin's Blow. The Champion ducked low but failed to clear the shield completely. The top of its head was caught by the improvised weapon and the Skill-driven blow rocked the monster backwards.

Panting with exertion, Daniel stepped forwards and kicked the monster directly in its chest to send the Champion sprawling backwards. Daniel then spun to the side to look over his companions. To his surprise, it was Omrak who most desperately needed his help, swarmed as the Northerner was by the Skeletons. Daniel rushed the monsters and triggered Double Strike again, each attack targeted at ripping a monster off the giant. He grimaced as an abrupt shift by the giant made one of his strikes glance off Omrak's arm, even as it ripped the skeleton off.

Freed at last, Omrak struggled to his knees. Enraged and glowing red, the Northerner pinned a Skeleton under one knee and pulled another down by gripping its pubic bone. On the ground, the monster was smashed repeatedly in its face by Omrak, cracking the orbital bone and finally shattering the skull in its entirety.

Daniel, his initial charge spent, proceeded to bend lower and push his shield into the midsection of a nearby Skeleton, pushing it away from Omrak and into the Champion. Crouched beneath his shield, Daniel proceeded to lash out at any opening he saw beneath his shield, crushing ankles and tibias as he spotted them. A sword flicked past the shield, coming at an angle and cutting deep into Daniel's side near his arm where his body was left unarmored. The attack forced his arm to collapse, the Skeleton he had been holding aloft crashing down on him.

Daniel tottered for a moment on his knees before he shrugged his shoulder and tossed the sprawled over monster behind him. The Champion stepped into the opening, a sword raised to plunge at Daniel's exposed throat. It was only a thrown knife that sliced through the air to crack into the monster's temple that threw the blow off to clatter uselessly off Daniel's armor.

Forcing what little strength he had into his knees, Daniel triggered Perin's Blow again, catching the Champion in the spine as he stood. The explosion of force threw the Champion backwards and left its spine broken. Daniel had no time to stop to gloat as he turned back to help his friends mop up the last of the monsters.

With the Champion broken and unable to continue fighting, the other monsters were quick to fall. Now that Omrak and Daniel were able to handle them, Asin scampered back with the remaining pair of Skeletons she had been distracting. Afterwards, the group sat in place, breathing deeply as they waited for the magical healing to slowly patch them together. Daniel grimaced, glancing at his remaining Mana pool, and walked over to Omrak, casting Minor Healing to help patch the open wound in his thigh. He would need to cast Healer's Mark at least a couple more times to heal the big man full which would significantly reduce his existing pool significantly. As it stood, he had used his Gift on the most serious of his own wounds to conserve Mana.

"Swords." Asin pointed at the pair of bone swords that lay on the ground.

"Omrak, can you carry them?" Daniel asked, gesturing to the weapons. The Northerner grimaced but walked over, picking up the pair and testing them.

"Good balance," Omrak stated. Touching a finger to the edges, he pulled his finger away with a whistle. "Still sharp."

"Could be good money," Daniel said, rubbing his chin.

Omrak nodded as he began to tie one sword to his own, electing to hold the second in hand. Asin, having recovered her breath, had pulled open the chest to reveal the floor stone. She held it aloft for everyone to see, a grin on her face. This was a stone she could be happy about.

"Better?" Daniel chuckled slightly and then winced, his ribs bruised from the repeated pounding. Better to get moving before they stopped for the day. Pulling himself to his feet, Daniel led the group to the next passageway, keeping his eye out for more skeletons. A short half-hour later, Daniel's eyes widened slightly as he received a notification as constant use of his healing skills finally resulted in an upgrade to its abilities. It did not take him much time to make the decision.

Minor Healing (I) upgraded to Minor Healing (II)

Heals minor wounds.

Effect: Heals Intelligence + Healing Skill level of wounds

Cost: 20 Mana

It was still an expensive spell, but it now healed a third more. It was comparable in terms of the amount healed now with Healer's Mark, but unlike Healer's Mark, which healed over a period of time, this was close to instantaneous. That was the reason Daniel decided to choose to upgrade this spell rather than Healer's Mark. One could keep them going on long delves, the other could save a life.

"Daniel," Omrak growled, bringing the Healer's attention back to the present. Daniel stared forwards, his attention drawn to the Skeletons stumbling forwards towards the party. They were in a small space here which meant there was no way for the monsters to flank them, but it also meant their continual screams would jar his nerves. Good thing they couldn't get past his armor. Settling into his stance, Daniel hefted his mace. No need to waste Stamina on special attacks here.

***

Seated in a larger cavern, the party rested their feet after a long day of searching. They had covered miles of underground passages, their only source of light the Mana lantern carried by Omrak. Miles of mapped passages behind them, the trio sat eating their meal together.

"How much more?" Omrak asked as he bit into his sandwich.

"No idea," Daniel said, looking up at the minimap. "Still, I think we're close. Maybe a few more hours if we are willing to continue pushing it."

"Tired," Asin growled, rubbing at her calves.

"There is danger in continuing without rest," Omrak said around a mouthful. "We risk running into further ambushes."

"True," Daniel said, frowning as he assessed his own body. He had less than a fifth of his Mana left and that needed to be held in reserve for combat. Fatigue ran through his muscles, his eyes bloodshot and aching from constant squinting. They could attempt to rest here, but the way the Skeletons roamed, it was unlikely to be a restful night. That left them one last option. He focused internally, pulling on his Gift and sending it coursing through his body. He felt his memory, his experience, slip from him as he washed the fatigue away.

Refreshed, Daniel walked over and placed a hand on Omrak's shoulder. A quick assessment made him blink—he had not even noticed the broken rib. That the Northerner had managed to walk and fight so long without complaint was amazing. Focusing, Daniel patched the rib and then cleared the chemical fatigue from Omrak's body, before doing the same for Asin.

"We good?" Daniel asked, stretching slowly. The physical exhaustion was wiped away, though the mental tiredness was still there, if lessened. A few more hours. He could do that, Daniel told himself.

"Aye. Thank you again, Hero Daniel," Omrak rumbled, and Asin nodded in agreement. Together, the trio stood and walked forwards into the darkness, a single light illuminating their way. In the clatter of their footsteps, Daniel wondered what new memory he had lost.

Chapter 12

"A Labyrinth." Daniel exhaled, staring at the maze that sprawled in front of them. As he had thought, it had only taken them another few hours to find the way down. However, as they poked their heads out of the entranceway of the staircase, all they could see was the start of the maze, its stone passageways spread out before them.

"This is what has held the Crimson Elms behind then," Omrak stated.

"Maze." Asin walked forwards, sniffing and eyeing the innocuous stone walls. Her fur ruffled slightly, and she paused before she took the next step, crouching and holding her hand above the gap between the two stone slabs on the ground.

"Trap," Daniel said before she could. He reached into a pouch and pulled a weighted ball, showing it to the Catkin. Asin quickly stepped back, nodding to Daniel. With an underhand toss, Daniel landed the ball on the stone slab, which flipped itself around, exposing a pit for a brief second.

"Seesaw trap," Omrak said, walking forwards and prodding the trap again to set it spinning.

"Yes," Asin said as she slowly moved along the edges of the trap to test the next stone piece. This one did not move. "More?"

Daniel frowned, mentally weighing his exhaustion. "No. We should go back."

"Test more," Asin said, moving forwards slowly as she prodded. "Extent."

"Not a good idea," Daniel said. "We're tired."

"Faster. Learn now."

"Daniel is right, Hero Asin, we are all exhausted," Omrak said.

"Asin …" Daniel started.

"No." Asin turned and glared at the duo. "More coin."

"Why, damn it?" Daniel stepped forwards and found himself stopping at the last second when he remembered the trap.

"Need," Asin said.

"So does Omrak. He doesn't even have armor and takes more damage than any of us," Daniel growled. "And he's saying we should go back."

"Show. Later," Asin finally huffed. "Test now."

Daniel gritted his teeth and then finally nodded. Fine. They would test the area for a bit, learn a little more about the labyrinth. But he wanted an answer.

"Tripwire. Darts."

"Deadfall. Spikes."

"Minotaur. Yours."

"Pitfall."

"Pressure. Fire."

A good hour and a half later, Daniel raised his hands as he called out, "Enough, Asin."

Asin paused, staring at Daniel, before she touched the pouch by her side. The Minotaurs were not particularly numerous, but it seemed the longer they stayed in the Labyrinth, the faster they came, tracking the group. Still, they were definitely more profitable with properly sized and lustrous Mana Stones. As for the traps, they had not found a new one recently.

"Okay," Asin relented, her tail no longer waving, her fur wilted.

"Finally," Omrak muttered, shaking his head as Daniel led the group back. Asin's ears twitched for a brief moment but stilled, the Catkin prowling behind the group as the trio edged around the marked traps.

"We coming back tonight?" Daniel asked. Inside the Dungeon, it was hard to tell the time, but it had to be early morning. By the time they had slept and woken up again, it would be late afternoon at best. Thankfully, the Dungeon made no difference if it was morning or evening.

"Yes." Asin nodded. "Need gear."

"We'll take some of today's earnings for the trap finders and more rope," Daniel said.

"Omrak. Buy?" Asin tilted her head to the side, looking up at the large Adventurer.

"I can do so. I believe I know what is necessary." Omrak nodded agreeably.

"Good."

Daniel blinked, having thought that he would be the one to do it. After all, that was what he normally did. He frowned slightly, wondering what it was all about, but then shrugged as he hopped over the trip wire. It did not matter, not really.

Still, he wondered.

***

"Daniel."

The knocking on the door woke Daniel from his sleep, making him groan. It felt like he had just gotten to sleep before he was woken. He stretched slowly, moving over to the water basin to splash his face, when another insistent knock disturbed his thoughts.

"Coming," Daniel called out around his washcloth. Grabbing his shirt, he shook his head to clear the cobwebs from his mind. Physically, there was just a residue of the exhaustion from yesterday. Mentally, though, he felt he could have spent another day in bed.

Pulling the door open, he saw Asin with her fist raised to knock again.

"Asin?" Daniel said, puzzled.

"Show," Asin said, before gesturing for Daniel to come. At his confusion, her tail twitched as she added, "Coin."

"This couldn't wait?" Daniel grumbled as he tucked his shirt in.

"No."

Daniel clamped his teeth around the words that threatened to spill out and walked back into his room to grab his mace and coin pouch from the bedstand before he walked with Asin down the stairs. He knew better than to push the Catkin to explain things before she was ready.

As they walked, Daniel glanced over at his friend, noting how her fur was still slightly wilted and not as well kept as usual. She moved with her usual grace but with a slight hitch in her steps that only someone who had spent as much time with the Catkin as he had would have noticed. Being both friend and her healer gave Daniel a unique insight into his party member he was coming to realize. As Daniel walked, he idly noted their route, realizing that he probably knew where they were going.

"Are we headed to the butcher?" Daniel asked, frowning.

"Yes," Asin answered before falling silent. She refused to answer any further questions, not even after she burdened Daniel down with the carcass of a pair of pigs, carrying a large bag herself too. After that, she threaded her way through the streets towards the Beastkin quarter.

"Am I just here to carry things for you?" Daniel grumped as he lurched behind the Catkin, carrying the meat.

"Wait."

The encumbered pair finally came up to a sprawling two-story building in the Beastkin quarter. Asin skipped past the main door immediately, leading him to a side door, which she proceeded to kick. When it opened, she handed her bag over to the large Bullkin inside, who gripped it and held a hand out to Daniel. Daniel frowned before handing his own burdens over, the glimpse of the inside detailing a large kitchen. The Bullkin snorted and growled afterwards to Asin, who yowled back, the pair holding a brief and noisy discussion before the door closed suddenly in their faces.

Finished, Asin turned away and gestured for Daniel to follow.

"Is that it?" Daniel asked, shaking his head. "That's your explanation? Meat to some building?"

"Yes." Asin stopped and pointed backwards. "School."

"You're feeding a school?" Daniel said slowly, frowning at her nod. "I'm going to need more than that."

"City no pay. No food. Children hungry. I buy," Asin said slowly, and exaggeratedly. "Expensive."

"How many children are in there?" Daniel asked as he reached for his pouch, his own generous nature tugging on him.

Asin hissed at him, stalking off.

"What?"

"Beastkin," Asin growled, and pointed around and then added, "Human. No help."

"Then why did you show this to me?" Daniel said.

"Insisted," Asin said as she turned back to her friend. "My problem. I deal. Tired now. Evening."

"Asin …" Daniel started and then fell silent, watching her walking away. Damn it, Asin.

Chapter 13

Labyrinths were a traditional level in most Dungeons, and depending on the level of the Dungeon, could sprawl over a few kilometers or tens of kilometers. However, no matter which level of Dungeon it was, the monster that inhabited it was the same—the Minotaur. Bipedal, seven-foot-plus monsters with muscles that rivalled Omrak's and a bull's face, they were equipped, or not, dependent on the Dungeon level. For a Beginner Dungeon like Karlak, the Minotaurs were unarmored and wielded copper swords and axes, which disappeared after their defeat.

Spinning around, Omrak swung his sword in a diagonal from his lower left to his right shoulder in a cut that battered aside the Minotaur's copper sword, tearing open its chest. Beside Omrak, Daniel fought much more guardedly, taking the Minotaur's strike on his shield and sliding it off to his left while he crushed the arm as the monster tried to retreat. Forced to drop the sword, the Minotaur backed away, swinging a hook that Daniel ducked beneath to continue his attack. Behind, Asin watched the pair fight as she ran her finger along the edge of a throwing knife, waiting.

"Thanks for the help," Daniel grumbled as he watched the Minotaur corpse disappear.

"Dangerous. Move bad," Asin explained, and then shrugged. "No need help."

"Aye, we required no help," Omrak said, picking up the Mana Stone and tossing it over to Asin to pocket. "Next trap?"

"Darts. Pressure and tripwire," Asin said, pointing down the hallway.

"Right," Omrak said, pulling out a ball to roll along the ground. Afterwards, he walked forwards slowly with the sword pushing ahead of him to trigger the tripwires.

Daniel followed along slowly as he stared at the map inside his head. The labyrinth was huge, and while they were following the time-honored tradition of staying to the left, it did mean they constantly found dead-ends. Interestingly enough, he had a nagging feeling that something was not right about this maze yet. It was a feeling that had yet to crystalize, which was why he kept silent, for now at least. Either way, there was a lot of ground to cover this evening.

***

A few hours later, the Catkin paused as she was about to take a step forwards. She pulled her leg back, crouching down as her ears twitched. In a moment, both Omrak and Daniel could hear it. A grinding noise that slowly increased in volume that seemed to surround them all.

"What is this?" Omrak growled, hands tense on his sword.

"The walls are moving," Daniel said, looking around himself. "The labyrinth is reshaping itself."

"Midnight," Asin guessed.

"Yes, probably. So that's why the Elms have been stuck," Daniel said, sighing. Between the traps and the shifting maze, each party had only a single day to attempt this.

"Problem. Out," Asin said, pointing back the way they came.

Daniel frowned, before he realized what she was saying. If the way back had changed, they were now lost in the middle of the maze without a way out. Or through. While the group obviously carried enough food for a few days, the possibility of getting stuck in the maze for all that time made Daniel shudder. It was a Miner's worst nightmare.

Both Asin and Omrak were silent as well as they considered the fact that now, they had no choice but to find a way out.

As the grinding and rumbling slowly came to an end, Daniel hitched up his bag, glanced at his friends, and said, "Let's go."

Nodding, Asin stepped forwards and started checking over the ground in front of them for traps. Omrak followed behind, watching for traps as well and monsters.

***

An hour later with no attacks, the trio glanced at each other. It was possible that the monsters had pulled back during the transformation and were only now filtering into the rest of the Dungeon. The other, more disturbing possibility was that they were actually cut off, their particular location within the Dungeon a completely enclosed route. It was a thought that none of the trio cared to share with their friends since there was nothing they could do about it. Still, the fear at the potential of being trapped, even for a day, made the trio move slightly faster than they should have.

Asin stepped forwards, placing her leg against the stone slab, and then found herself tipping forwards as the slab slipped open beneath her weight. Pitched forwards, she threw her hands backwards in a futile attempt to stop her plunge. Only a desperate grab by Omrak on her cloak halted her fall before he yanked her to safety.

Yowling in distress, Asin rubbed at her throat where the rough handling had bruised it. Still, she nodded her thanks to Omrak. The giant Northerner did not notice this, having edged over to stare at the slab of stone while he wedged it open with his sword. Surprisingly, instead of a simple deadfall, the edges of the trap were filled with spikes that were certain to injure any unlucky Adventurer. Thankfully, it was not a large fall, just under six feet. Not lethal, but painful.

"You okay?" Daniel asked.

Asin nodded slightly as she tried to control her breathing and slow her heart. Eventually, she stood up and walked around the edge of the trap, ready to test for the next section. Unfortunately, the Dungeon had no easily discernable ratio of traps to corridor, which meant each section had to be checked carefully.

"We can take a break if you want?" Daniel called out after her as he brought up the back.

Rather than answer him directly, Asin just continued to move forwards slowly.

It was a relief when they eventually ran into a group of Minotaurs. The Minotaur group had just turned the corner and, on spotting the trio, roared before they charged. The lead Minotaur stumbled slightly as it hoof caught a tripwire, righting itself soon after and continuing the charge. Daniel growled at the unfairness of it all as the trap refused to trigger. Asin in the front stood up swiftly, drawing and throwing her knife and activating her ability Fan of Knives at the same time. Knives split again and again, plunging into the monster's body.

Injured, the Minotaur next ran into Omrak and his sword. Raised above his head, Omrak suddenly stepped forwards and swung the sword down, splitting its skull open between its horn. Daniel finally managed to get his crossbow loaded, the newly released bolt catching a Minotaur right above its hip and spinning it about with the force of impact. His crossbow empty,

Daniel dropped the weapon and ran forwards to meet the remaining half dozen with mace and shield.

Asin continued to harass the monsters with her knives, dancing to the side with each attack. A thrown knife spun through the air, sparks of electricity dancing as it lodged in a Minotaur's bicep, forcing its attack on Omrak askew. Daniel Shield Bashed an incoming attack, the powered block ripping the sword from a monster's hand before Daniel began his series of attacks.

A few minutes later, the trio were left panting amongst the shiny blue sparkles of light as the corpses dispersed. Recovered, Daniel walked over to Omrak to cast Healer's Mark and bandage his ribs where a cut had opened up. No point in stitching it; the spell would fix the damage soon enough. Or, as Daniel eyed his friend, perhaps the second use of the spell.

Asin limped over and prodded Daniel, pointing to the cuts on her thigh and upper arm in order. At the end, she had been forced to jump into melee combat to ensure an injured Minotaur did not flank the pair. Unfortunately, the huge height and strength difference had left the Catkin at a serious disadvantage.

Still, for all their injuries, the fight had lifted the mood of the group. Fighting for their lives was a danger that the trio were used to. Slowly starving to death, trapped underground was not for Asin and Omrak. As for Daniel, it was a danger that he had thought he had left behind. Grinning slightly at each other, the trio collected the Mana Stones and moved on.

***

The good news, thought Daniel, was that they were definitely not trapped in a portion of the labyrinth by the shifting of the walls. At least, if they were trapped, the portion they were trapped in was huge. The bad news was that, even after four hours, the party still had not found a way out. Since each corridor was the same, there really was no way to tell if the exit was around the next corner or a hundred corners from now.

By now, the thrill of the initial fight had gone away, and even subsequent fights had not brought any of the excitement back. Now, it was just the slow grind of checking for traps, walking along blue-tinted corridors and the occasional, hectic fights.

A sullen silence had fallen among the group as they concentrated on their respective tasks. Daniel scanned for trouble ahead and behind them, while Asin checked for traps, and Omrak watched her and marked the traps they found. Occasional grunts and whispered words of warning were the only sounds that emanated from the group, as they plodded through the labyrinth.

Eventually, it was Omrak who broke the silence. "Is this the same passage? Again?"

"Yes," Daniel said, pointing down to the third of four passages that split from here.

"Did we just walk in a circle," Omrak growled, hands tightening on his sword.

"Yes," Daniel answered again while Asin crept forwards, prodding at a suspicious stone. A hiss and a dart flew out from the side, striking the stone on the opposite wall. The Catkin did not even blink, just edged to the left to test the next stone.

"Are you sure about your map?" Omrak asked, leaning forwards.

"Yes," Daniel replied again.

"Stop it. You can speak in full sentences," Omrak snapped, stomping his foot.

"Why?" Daniel paused and then added, "There's nothing else to say. We just need to keep walking."

"For how long? We've been down here for hours now. We can't even tell how long," Omrak said, waving a hand at the enclosed corridors. "It'd be at least seven, eight hours."

"Yes," Daniel said, stretching. "Do you want to take a break? We probably have the rest of the day."

"A break. I just want out!" Omrak snarled. "I want to stop walking around in a circle. I want to know we're actually getting somewhere."

Asin scurried to the side, a hand touching the top of a throwing knife as her eyes narrowed at the raging giant. Daniel stared at Omrak, opened his mouth and then shut it before he finally tried again. "I can't guarantee we can get out. But we are getting somewhere. Slowly."

"We only have your map to tell us," Omrak said, gritting his teeth. "What if you die. What if you get hurt or separated? What happens to us then?"

Daniel started to answer and then paused, actually considering Omrak's words. Finally, he said, "You're correct. We'll take a break and I'll draw a map for us."

Omrak, mollified, finally nodded and flopped to the floor before he reached for his pack to find something to eat. Asin took a seat as well, pulling her waterskin to sip at it. Better to drink slowly—relieving oneself in a Dungeon was never enjoyable. Daniel rubbed his temple as he dug out some parchment and some charcoal to sketch the map that he saw in his head. A part of him, a deep part of him, resented having to do this. However, Daniel squashed the emotions as he worked on the paper. Omrak was right. They definitely did not want to get lost—even if they were following the old wall-following rule, it was no guarantee that they would find the exit that way.

Better to sketch the map, know where they were going, and if they finally found themselves where they started again, they would at least have a map to start from. As it stood, they had already investigated two different islands on the chance that the stairways down were in them.

Daniel was fast beginning to understand why multi-week trips into Dungeon levels were a thing. It had been hard to grasp the complexity of exploring Dungeons before, but being trapped inside the Labyrinth—even if it was for only a few hours—was a definite learning experience. Twenty-five minutes later, Daniel finished the parchment and handed it to Omrak.

"Keep it. Mark it as we go along," Daniel added, and Omrak nodded grimly. The big Northerner opened his mouth to say something else and then shut it, shaking his head.

***

The echoing roar made the trio shift in their steps again before they glanced at one another. Asin snarled slightly but moved forwards again to the next set of paving stones. That roar, louder and more challenging than ever, had been echoing through the corridors for the last half-hour, getting slowly closer and closer. Slowly was the pertinent word, though.

"Closer. A lot closer," Omrak muttered, sliding the map back into his pouch.

Daniel nodded, putting his mace back into its loop in his belt before he picked up his crossbow. He cranked the crossbow back and slid a bolt in now that he knew they were likely to meet the screamer soon. Then perhaps they would find out who it was, though Daniel had his suspicions.

Asin nearly had the entire passageway cleared before she paused, sniffing the air. She waved the group back even as she drew more knives. It did not take long before the other two heard what Asin had smelled already—company was coming.

Three Minotaurs and a Minotaur Champion walked around the corner, weapons held in their hands. As a group, the Minotaurs rushed forwards while the Champion, standing half a foot taller and nearly the same again wide, rushed forwards while letting loose an all too familiar scream. Daniel hissed, his crossbow raised and firing even as the throwing axe and throwing knives took their attackers in the chest. Daniel's jaw dropped as he watched the Champion pull one of its compatriots into the path of his bolt before he let it go, letting the injured Minotaur stagger back to its feet, clutching its arm.

Omrak surged ahead as he picked up his sword from the passage, holding it diagonally as he charged. As he neared, he swung it, a glowing yellow light filling the blade. A hasty block by his target did nothing to slow the unstoppable cut, the Minotaur's blade shattering as it connected with Omrak's glowing weapon. A moment later, the Minotaur's body was bisected as well.

Asin cursed as a second Piercing Shot was dodged by the Minotaur Champion as it bore down on her. He was stopped only by Daniel, who lunged forwards, triggering a Shield Bash. The Champion twisted at the last second, taking the strike in his shoulder and staggering backwards. Given a bit of space, Daniel stepped quickly to the right and struck with Perin's Blow at another Minotaur, sending it crashing into the wall.

Omrak grunted his thanks even as he sidestepped quickly, dodging a strike from his opponent while he cut at its leg. The Minotaur snarled as its muscles gave way while Omrak doubled down on his attack. Behind, Asin threw her knives at the Minotaur Daniel had hurt, keeping it from rejoining the fight.

Daniel turned back around to meet the Champion, catching a downwards strike on his shield. He found himself driven to his knee by the attack, the blow hard enough that his entire arm collapsed backwards to hit him on his head. Even before he could stand, the Minotaur Champion was slamming its sword down again, forcing Daniel to stay on his knees and reinforce his shield arm with his other hand.

Asin spotted the difficulty that Daniel was in and whipped a Fan of Knives at the Champion, the knives sinking into its body. The attack provided Daniel a moment to scramble backwards. As he stood, Daniel attempted to raise his shield arm and failed, the constant blows having dislocated it and his attempts at moving send fresh pain shooting through his body. The Champion, having recovered from Asin's attack, lowered its head and charged Daniel, closing in on him quickly. Daniel ducked sideways, dodging the charge mostly and hitting the monster as it passed.

Turning around quickly, the Champion shifted, putting Daniel in the way of Asin's knife, which clattered off his backplate as he stepped to keep himself in front of the monster. Daniel blinked, startled by the noise and impact, a moment's distraction that let the Champion roar and swing its sword forwards, its blow catching on Daniel's left pauldron. He groaned, the impact bruising his body again.

Asin, snarling, backed up to give herself more space to throw her knives. She sent them overhand, the knives arcing over the top of Daniel's head to target the Champion, who bobbed and weaved. Seeing the monster distracted, Daniel lunged low and triggered Perin's Blow against the monster's knee, feeling it crack as the knee gave way. Standing swiftly, Daniel then triggered a pair of strikes to finish the monster off while Asin sank a couple of electrified knives into its body. Crippled, the Champion did its best to fend off the joint attacks but finally collapsed, leaving Daniel panting from deep exhaustion.

Omrak, having finished his own opponents, stared down at the monsters and the bruised Daniel, shaking his head.

"A great opponent," Omrak rumbled.

"Urgh." Daniel groaned, leaning against a wall as he healed himself.

"Well, at least I'm not the one injured this time," Omrak said, grinning. He frowned suddenly, twisting to the side as lights began to play along the ground. "What's that?"

The pair just shook their heads, staring at the lights and gripping their weapons. They only relaxed when the lights stopped glowing to reveal a familiar treasure chest. Asin grinned, skipping over to open it, while Daniel sank back down, feeling the dislocated shoulder slowly grinding back into place.

Even after he healed, they still had to find a way out.

Chapter 14

It was probably, by Daniel's estimation, an hour past noon. It was hard to tell of course without the sun, but having been a Miner before, Daniel had gained some skill at guessing such things. The group had finally decided that it was best to rest for a few hours after Asin had been speared in the leg from a trap she had missed. After healing her, Daniel was completely out of Mana, and further attempts at exploration from the exhausted party had been left for later.

In an attempt to ensure their safety, the party had backtracked to a single, relatively trap-free corridor and set up camp in its center. After a hurried discussion, both Asin and Omrak bedded down while Daniel refreshed himself with his Gift. He would, in a few hours, take a nap himself to refresh his mind, but his Gift left him able to withstand the rigors of the Dungeon better. Now, if only he could remember what it was that had left him when he had activated his Gift. Somehow, Daniel knew that the memory was important.

Shaking his head, Daniel chewed on the beef jerky as he watched both sides. His crossbow lay next to him, fully loaded and ready for use. Alone with his thoughts and the insistent snoring of the Catkin, Daniel could only sit on watch, attempting to keep himself from falling asleep.

This was their first true test as a party with Omrak in it and, thus far, Daniel felt things were going well. Sort of. Everyone was short-tempered, and the once talkative Northerner had slowly grown more and more sullen. That actually helped, since Daniel knew that Asin found the constant chatter annoying, so Omrak growing silent helped her not lose her temper. The only downside was that Omrak's temper was somewhat more volatile, but it could be worse.

Eyes half-closed, Daniel blinked as he heard the clink and scrape of movement. He reached for his crossbow, waiting for the noise to resolve itself. Eventually, the noise faded, and Daniel leaned back, resting once more. It was going to be a long few hours.

***

"Mmmmpphfff…" Daniel groaned, rolling to his feet. He'd only had a half-hour of rest as it stood, and his head felt worse than before, filled with wool and grit. Still, they could not waste any more time. They needed to complete this level before it reset.

"Coffee?" Omrak offered Daniel the mug as he stood up.

"Thank you." Daniel sipped on the mug and then blinked, staring at the warm mug. He frowned, looking around and not seeing the fire. "How …?"

"Northerner secret," Omrak said, grinning hugely. "Drink up. We should begin."

Daniel glared at how chipper Omrak was but fell silent, deciding to just drink up and enjoy the unexpected luxury. In a few moments the group was packed and on their way back to where they last left off, searching for the way down or the exit.

An hour later, Asin's ears twitched. She held a hand up, calling the group to a stop as she listened to the voices. Frowning, she tapped her ears and then waited for the pitiful humans to finally hear what she did.

Seeing that the Catkin did not seem perturbed, the pair waited patiently. Soon enough, they picked out the voices in conversation before the Crimson Elms came walking out from a side corridor. Leading the group was the short, quiet man from before and, directly behind him, staff held aloft, was the Mage. His staff was glowing red and where the light fell, traps that were hidden glowed.

"Cheating," Asin muttered, and Daniel could only nod. Still, the pair were quick to note where the traps on this corridor were. No reason to not make use of the unexpected bonus.

"Well, look who it is. We heard you might be down here," Amrah said, her eyes dancing over the trio scornfully.

"Heroes," Omrak greeted them with a smile, absently tucking away their map. "Did you just enter?"

"Of course not," Amrah said, snorting, and then raked her eyes over the disheveled group. "Get caught in the change?"

"Yes," Daniel said, stepping forwards as he eyed the other group. "Are you charting your way in?"

"Of course." Amrah smirked. The larger fighter said nothing, just watching the group while the Mage tapped his staff on the ground impatiently.

"Amrah, we should be moving along," Harald said. Amrah glanced at the staff again and nodded, moving to walk past the group.

Daniel, however, stepped sideways slightly, blocking their way as he cleared his throat. "We were actually hoping you could share your map. It'd help us get out."

Amrah frowned and then glanced to Harald, who shook his head. Daniel grimaced and stepped aside without being asked to. The Crimson Elms moved right past the group, stepping between the Adventurers and, in the shorter fighter's case, brushing against Omrak as he walked past. The party stayed silent, watching them leave, before the group headed down the corridor, skipping past the traps that had been highlighted.

"That's the way out ..." Daniel said, pointing to the way the Elms had come from.

"Eventually," Omrak said, rubbing his chin. "Probably."

"Definitely. Though, it'd take a while to get there," Daniel added.

"No, go on," Asin said, pointing down the corridor.

"We've been in here for a while," Daniel said as he surveyed the tired group.

"No. Go on," Asin said, shaking her head. When Daniel started to look mulish, she pointed down the way they came and which the Elms had continued on.

"Bad. Probably." Since they had started from within the Dungeon, there was no guarantee that the way they had not gone was not the way out.

"Bad." She pointed again to where the Elms had come from.

"Good." Asin pointed.

"Hero Asin is correct," Omrak said. "It would be wrong for us to give up now. The Elms have actually reduced the area we must search."

"We are assuming they did their job properly," Daniel muttered. Asin nodded and then pointed again down the corridor.

"Voted."

"Fine," Daniel grumped, shaking his head. It seemed they were going to do or die then. Well, preferably not die.

It was a short five minutes before they reached the next turn. Omrak reached into his pouch and then stopped, groping the leather pouch. He frowned, searching again, and then he pulled it from his belt to turn it inside out.

"Something wrong?" Daniel asked, even as Asin worked on the next corridor on the right.

"The map. It is gone," Omrak said.

"Did you drop it?"

"No. I put it in my pouch," Omrak said slowly. "I drew in the corridor on the right. Just before the Elms arrived."

"The Elms ..." Daniel frowned, his eyes widening. That shorter fighter, he had brushed up against Omrak. "He didn't, did he?"

"I believe the Elms are less than heroic," Omrak said, growling softly. "I do not believe I dropped it."

"Should we ...?" Daniel muttered, staring backwards. If they had the map, they would be able to skip to the end where the group had started exploring. Daniel stared up at the map in his head, mentally judging distances. After a few minutes, he swore softly. Assuming they did not have to face any Minotaurs, the Elms could reach the end of the map in two or three hours of straight walking. If they decided to, they would only have to check out the opposite direction that the team had chosen not to explore.

"Damn it," Daniel swore softly. This would give them a huge lead. Of course, the question would be if the staircase was down that way. Or the Elms could wait and backtrack and follow behind Daniel and his team, searching down this part of the maze using the same assumption that Daniel and his team were using to skip the Elm's route.

"Trap," Asin called out.

"Asin, did you hear …?" Daniel said.

"Yes. Trap," Asin reiterated, and pointed downwards before stepping over the trap to check on the next stone.

Omrak stared at the Catkin and then opened his mouth before he shut it. His lips twisted as he stared back to where the Elms had left, before he turned to Daniel, opening his mouth. Daniel on the other hand shook his head, cutting Omrak off. The Northerner growled, but subsided as he realized he was outvoted.

Damn it. But Asin was right—confronting the group would do nothing. Better to focus on what they needed to do.

***

Blood running down his arm, Omrak roared as he tackled the Minotaur that had cut him. Falling down together, he scrambled up the monster's body, holding its arm down as he began to land punch after punch into its face, knuckles tearing skin and fur. Behind, Asin ducked beneath a strike and lashed out again with her knives, cutting the tendons in the Minotaur's elbow before she lunged forwards, opening the wound wider. Daniel, hunkered beneath his shield, fought his own opponent more carefully, trading strikes.

A short few minutes later, the trio stood victorious staring at the staircase down. They had found it, finally. Not without running into this last batch of monsters.

"Ready?" Daniel asked. Omrak nodded but Asin just stared into space, growling softly to herself as her tail waved lazily.

"Asin?"

"Busy," Asin hissed before continuing to stare into space.

"I believe she has Leveled Up," Omrak offered, and Daniel nodded in belated agreement.

Well, they could wait. The pair moved aside to sit down while they waited for Asin to be done. Idly, Omrak took his sword out and began to clean it and, after a moment, Daniel followed his example to care for his own gear.

"I noticed you have a new ability," Daniel said to fill the silence.

"Yes, I gained it last Level," Omrak said. "The Fangs of Zemur."

"You don't use it often."

"It requires significant amounts of Stamina. My father always said to use such abilities sparingly."

"Ah …" Daniel fell silent. "Your father was an Adventurer?"

"No. A farmer."

"Oh …"

"In the North, all are taught to fight. We are not numerous and so all must enter the Dungeons to quell the monsters. My father ventured into many before he gained his name and inherited the land from his father."

"I never really knew mine," Daniel said, feeling a familiar ache in his chest at that thought.

"My condolences."

"It's fine," Daniel said before he fell silent. Omrak, sensing the mood that Daniel was in, focused on caring for his blade. After a time, Asin finally nodded to herself. The pair stood up, walking to her.

"What did you get?" Daniel asked curiously.

"Serpent's Tooth," Asin said. "Poison."

"Oh …" Daniel frowned. He was not entirely sure he liked that answer. Poison could be helpful, but if one of them got injured by it, it could make things more difficult. He certainly had no spell to cure poison. Still, it did shore up one of Asin's major weaknesses, which was her inability to inflict significant amount of damage. At least, he thought so.

"Well, we good to go?" Daniel asked, and after receiving the confirming nods, the trio trooped down the stairs. Finally, they would be able to exit this level and the Dungeon. Best of all—this left them in the lead again.

Chapter 15

"Three more floors at most," Khy'ra said, smiling softly at her boyfriend. He lay lounging on the bed, holding her hand as she sat next to him.

"That's right," Daniel said.

"Do you know what you're going to do when you're done? There's a lot more Advanced Dungeons and a few Beginner ones close by too."

"Mmmm … I was thinking that Peel might be good to finish. It shouldn't be too hard, and we know about it already," Daniel said. "I haven't spoken to Asin or Omrak about their plans."

"Always good to ask your party members," Khy'ra chuckled.

"I don't know if Asin would come with us, though," Daniel said, grimacing. Omrak, Daniel was pretty certain would be happy to come.

"The school?"

"You know?" Daniel asked, surprised. After a brief moment's consideration, Daniel realized that of course the Elf would know. Khy'ra was an important part of the city and spoke with a wide range of citizens everyday. "It's important to her. And if she left …"

"There wouldn't be anyone helping out," Khy'ra finished for him.

"She wasn't doing this before, was she?" Daniel said, and Khy'ra shook her head.

"The Council cut the budget when the Dungeon was closed. Said they couldn't afford it anymore."

"But the Dungeon's open again."

"Oh Daniel." Khy'ra smiled softly at her boyfriend. "It's never that easy. They've been wanting to cut it for ages. This was just an excuse."

"Is there … is there anything I can do?"

To this, Daniel received a quick kiss on the head. "If I think of anything …"

"Tell me," Daniel said. He knew Asin had told him not to get involved, but this seemed so unfair. However, he could think of nothing that he could do—he did not even know where to start to help. A city budget was not something you could hit or delve. And contributing to the school, well, it was a short-term solution.

***

A day later, the group found themselves on level eight, staring at a familiar vista. The trio glanced at one a nother before laughing, walking forwards into the large caverns. As Daniel stared at the map in his head, he laughed softly. This was literally the same level eight as before the Dungeon had changed its configuration.

Feeling more relaxed, Daniel directed the group down to where they last left off and the staircase to the ninth level, glad to finally be on familiar ground once again.

***

With a grace that belied his stature, Omrak ducked beneath the Ogre's club and swung his sword in a short horizontal strike that ended in the monster's knee. Twisting his blade, the Northerner ripped it upwards, opening a wider wound on the creature's thigh. Using the impetus of standing, Omrak kicked forwards and sent the injured Ogre sprawling backwards before he reset himself for his next opponent.

"Should we help him?" Daniel asked, having dispatched his own Ogre.

Asin shook her head, squatting on the corpse of the Ogre she had stabbed in the eyes. The giant Northerner had rushed forwards to meet the first group of six ogres on his lonesome, wielding his sword and screaming with battlelust. Omrak had dispatched the first Ogre with his new Skill before he was bogged down fighting the others. It was only the arrival of the pair that stopped him from being flanked. Omrak, however, did not seem intent on sharing the last three monsters at all, wide strikes and frenzied darting ensuring neither Adventurer could close in and aid him safely.

Not that he needed it. Daniel winced as Omrak lopped off a hand and then, on the return cut, opened up the Ogre's stomach. The Northerner seemed to revel in the open space and monstrous opponents, wielding his sword with wild abandon. The incidental wounds he picked up just added to the strength of his attacks. In truth, this was a horrible match for the Dungeon. Not only did the wide-open caverns that made up the Ogre floor allow Daniel to use his plate armor and crossbow to full effect, the numerous monsters allowed Omrak to unleash the full range of his fighting style. Even Asin, with her new Skill, could contribute to the fight. The group was tearing through the floor like Asin's chili and Omrak's guts.

***

That evening, when the trio emerged, they did so with smiles on their faces. Not only had the party cleared the Ogres without a problem, the Mana Stones each of the Ogres dropped was of good value and as frequent as the attacks. They had even inadvertently managed to stumble upon the Ogre Champion and the floor chest, a battle that had ended with Daniel spending nearly half his Mana patching up the stubborn Northerner, who had traded blows with the Champion till one fell. It was quite apparent to Daniel that the group had grown stronger during their time through the new Dungeon. The fact that they knew what traps, what terrain, and what tactics to expect had made the floor so much simpler than their previous experience on this floor. In addition, Daniel could not help but smile at the fact that he had now reached Level 9.

In a good mood, the party tramped into the Adventurers' Guild to drop their day's earnings off with Liev.

"Good day?" Liev asked, noticing the smiling group. Quick nods from all three made him return the smile before he sobered up. He hated to tell them this, but it had to be done.

"The Crimson Elms were just in. They've cleared the eighth floor too."

The trio stared at Liev, their good mood suddenly deflated.

"How?" Daniel said.

"It's not a hard floor," Liev said, lips twisting slightly. "No puzzles, no difficult traps, no mazes. And they bought the map to it since the layout didn't change at all."

"Oh ..." Daniel groaned and rubbed his temples. There were only two floors left that were possible and the last floor might just be a Boss Monster.

Asin growled, tugging on Daniel's arm. She pointed back the way they came to the Dungeon entrance. Daniel shook his head automatically, already mentally assessing his Mana stores and the weariness in his body.

"No, Asin," Daniel said. "I just used most of my Mana healing us before we came up. There's daring and then there's reckless. This is reckless."

Omrak watched the pair argue, his hand absently stroking the hilt of his pommel.

"Quest," Asin said, her tail lashing out behind her.

"It's a whole floor. Maybe two. We've never fought a Dungeon Boss either, Asin," Daniel growled, shaking his head. "No. It's too dangerous."

"Try," Asin said again, pointing.

"No," Daniel said.

Omrak, watching the two, cleared his throat. "Perhaps, Heroes, I might offer a suggestion."

Daniel and Asin both shot a glare at the youngster before they paused, remembering that he was a part of the party. Daniel nodded jerkily and Omrak smiled at the two.

"Let us rest for a few hours. Tomorrow at dawn, we can begin and not leave till we complete the quest. It will give Hero Daniel time to recover his Mana and us to gather what supplies we need," Omrak said.

"That's …" Daniel began and then stopped, shrugging. "That's reasonable."

Asin growled, looking unhappy, but she finally nodded.

"Liev, can we use our earnings to purchase some of the Healing potions the Guild stocks?" Daniel asked.

"Of course," the redheaded attendant said, smiling slightly at the group as he busied himself with sorting the last of the stones.

"Also, there's something strange about the ninth floor," Daniel said, lowering his floor. "Tell me what you think about this …"

***

The ninth-floor annex looked like every other annex they had seen thus far, a simple carved stone room illuminated by Mana-imbued stone. Daniel hefted his mace, rolling his shoulders as he banished his doubts concerning their plan. If they pushed through on this floor, perhaps they had a chance to win the quest rewards. Waking up early in the morning, packing for a multiple-day delve, this was the last roll of the die for them.

When the group stepped out, familiar underground cave corridors awaited them. The corridors and caverns were a mix of natural and sentient carved surfaces that sprawled outwards, passages and exits leading not only from ground level but ten or twenty feet up, all illuminated by the lightest of Mana-imbuing. Some of the exits were blocked by familiar grey- and brown-colored walls, while the slightly acrid smell of Ixillian Crawlers' chemically altered saliva permeated the air.

"Remember, they're likely to be just the harassers," Daniel muttered, staring at the walls. It was the only explanation that Liev could come up with, that the Crawlers were being reused to provide cover for something more dangerous. Daniel sighed, shifting slightly in his leather armor as he committed the room to memory. Knowing what they were walking into, he had downgraded to his lighter and less bulky armor for the most part. Sadly, his enchanted bracers had been sold, leaving him wearing his iron bracers. Still, at least this way he was less likely to get stuck.

"Let us begin," Omrak growled, shifting his backpack to settle more comfortably behind him.

With a nod, Asin led the way, choosing one of the initially larger passages. Past experience had told them to be wary of traps on these levels, so leaving the Catkin to lead was the smart choice. Past experience had also indicated that what started out as a large passageway might easily become something a lot smaller.

It was a bare five minutes before they encountered their first monster. It oozed from a cavern ceiling as they walked, landing with a splash on top of Daniel. Immediately, the slime's acidic body began to eat into Daniel's armor, its body flowing around his protection to burn his skin. Daniel's shout of surprise was enough to warn the other two, which allowed Asin's quick reactions to dodge another falling monster. Omrak was not as lucky, the creature having missed the Northerner's torso but still managing to wrap a flailing appendage around his thigh. Unlike Daniel's, Omrak's began to let loose a series of light shocks, making the big Adventurer's thigh muscles clench and release.

Daniel swiped at the slime on his shoulder, his gloved hand brushing through the monster and doing no damage. He frantically tried again as the creature burned through his flesh, setting his nerves alight. Omrak, knife in hand, swiped at the main body of the creature attacking him with as little success. It was only Asin who managed to hurt her opponent. A thrown blade passed through a slime body, sending sparks of electricity shooting through it. Left behind by the blade were traces of poison that began to discolor the purple gelatinous monster, tendrils of green creeping deeper and deeper through the gelatinous body. The purple monster shook and shuddered at the attack, lurching forwards in its attempt to attack the Catkin.

Daniel saw none of that, his focus on the monster on his shoulder. As he swiped again at the creature, something caught his eye. A small, floating blue stone within the creature. Inspiration struck and on his next attack, he reached out and grabbed the stone that attempted to float aside. Too close and too spread out on his body to get away, the stone was easily grasped and pulled from the slime. In a moment, the entire slime's body broke apart without its core, falling away from Daniel's body.

"The stones. Destroy the stones!" Daniel shouted in relief.

Heeding Daniel's advice, Omrak attacked the slime's glowing core. Unlike Daniel's, though, this monster had only laid a few tendrils on the Northerner and, as such, was better able to dodge and shift its stone. Eventually, Omrak landed a blow that shattered the stone and ended the monster.

"Bad. Destroy stone," Asin muttered, pointing at Omrak's. Her own slime had expired from the poison and repeated shocks shortly before Omrak's.

"It was killing me," hissed Omrak.

"Yes. Not dead, good," Asin said, and pointed to the stones. "Less coin, bad."

Daniel ignored the pair arguing, his hand on his own shoulder as he cast his Healer's Mark on himself. Silently, he assessed the damage with his Gift and hissed at the results. In the short battle, the acid slime had eaten not only through his skin but into some of the underlying muscle and nerves itself. Daniel gritted his teeth and focused, healing nerves and muscles before stopping. Better to let the spell finish the job.

"Slimes," Daniel said finally, rejoining the conversation that had finally stalled between the other two Adventurers. "Is there another way to kill them?"

"Poison. Electricity," Asin said.

"Neither of which Omrak or I have," Daniel pointed out.

"Fire?" Omrak said, touching his backpack. "I have torches."

"Wet." Asin pointed to where the slime had been, the body having dispersed.

"True, but we might as well try it," Daniel said, nodding to Omrak, who was already pulling out a torch from his backpack. At least with his mace, he had a better chance of hitting the stone than Omrak with his knife or sword. When Omrak had the torch lit, Daniel jerked his head to Asin and the group started off. Now that they knew what to expect, the imposing ninth floor seemed less threatening. Dangerous, lethal, but less threatening.

***

Fire worked. Sort of. It was not a strong weapon—a torch thrust at a slime could burn it, hurt it, but you also risked the torch being extinguished. Omrak soon learnt that it was actually better for him to almost hit a slime, to keep the torch close to the body and let the heat that emanated from the torch do its job, rather than stabbing it in like a sword. It was not perfect; it was in fact nearly as ineffective as using his bladed weapons. Nearly.

At least they were not fighting a fire slime. Exploration over the last few hours had made it clear that there were a multitude of different forms of slime present on the ninth level. Each carried its own danger—fire slimes spat out flaming portions of its body that refused to die off and exploded upon death. Earth slimes carried numerous rocks within their body, giving the slime the potential to strike and defend itself from Daniel's mace. Air slimes no longer crawled, spread, or glooped their way, but floated through the air in an attempt to enclose and suffocate.

And of course, the Crawlers made their presence known, sometimes at the most inopportune times. Armored carapaces that crawled through the Dungeons, walling off sections and attacking with little care for their lives. They were not deadly if taken on alone, but when combined with the slimes which were resistant to most normal attacks, had proven a dangerous combination.

Daniel shook his head as he surveyed the surroundings while Asin explored the cavern they had exited into. The Catkin as always was checking for new traps, though thus far, there were none but the usual pitfalls, which were easy enough to avoid. Behind, Daniel could hear pained grunts as Omrak pulled himself along the final narrow passageway. For some reason, the Crawlers never finished sealing the passages, leaving the Adventurers a small but tight exit. Tight enough that the large Northerner was finding it difficult to squirm his way out.

"Do you need help?" Daniel said for the third time.

"I shall manage, Hero," Omrak grunted out, his voice strained.

"Okay then." Daniel fell silent again, letting his gaze roam over the surroundings, wary of another attack. The slimes did not wait around like other monsters, roaming from cavern to cavern and seeming to prefer ambushes rather than straight fights. With their gelatinous bodies, they could squirm through the smallest cracks and appear without warning.

"Aaaarrrgghhh ..." Omrak roared as he shoved his arm and shoulder through the gap and grasped a convenient stalagmite. Gripping it tight, he pulled his body again, wide shoulders stuck on the edges. His shirt, abused once too often, tore, and the Northerner found himself swearing.

Daniel, his attention drawn to the partially exited giant, never saw the swarm of Air Slimes float down from a passageway high up in the ceiling. They made no sound as they controlled the winds around them, the group of five slimes splitting off with one going after Omrak and two others for the free pair.

It was only the shift in air currents that gave Daniel a fraction of a moment's warning. He shifted to the side, shield rising and bashing the slime away. He jumped back quickly as the second slime swooped in on him and then raised his shield up to Bash it. He surged forwards and his shield smashed the slime backwards, sending the gelatinous blob to smack into a cavern wall. That dealt with, Daniel spun around, only to have to throw himself backwards in an ungraceful sprawl as the monster attempted to land on his face again.

Asin, on the other hand, took a more direct route, sprinting around the cavern and throwing her knives at the monsters. Each attack sent dancing sparks of electricity and purple streaks of poison, injuring the monsters that attempted to catch the elusive Catkin. As she darted right past Daniel, she swiped a clawed hand at the monster that attacked him and then sprinted to where Omrak, unable to protect himself, was struggling against his own slime. Caught unawares, the slime had engulfed his face and pushed a part of itself down his mouth before he could stop it.

Daniel snarled, ducking under another swoop by the slime that attacked him before he spun and lashed out with his mace. It caught and ripped a glob off it, missing the all-important core however. Dancing to the side again, Daniel was forced to bob and weave as he attempted to hit the core again and again.

The fast-moving, darting monsters were hard to hit as they attempted to land on the Adventurers. Forced to duck and swipe, it was Asin's slimes that finally expired first from repeated exposures to lightning and poison. The Catkin paused, scanning the surroundings, and snarled, seeing that Omrak was no longer struggling. She darted over, claws appearing in her hands as she scrabbled around the slime, before finally succeeding at pulling the core out. Almost immediately, the slime dissolved, but Omrak did not move.

Asin snarled and slapped the big Adventurer in the face. Omrak did not react at all and the Catkin spun, already calling for Daniel. Daniel Bashed his last slime with his shield, this time managing to force its core from its body, killing it. Freed, Daniel looked to Asin and then Omrak, his eyes widening.

The healer darted forwards, a hand outstretched to touch the large Adventurer's still body. The moment contact was made, he sent his Gift into Omrak's body. Lips tense, he noted that the large Northerner was no longer breathing, though his heart still beat. Only a single surge of power was needed before Omrak gasped out loud, his body forced to breathe again.

Asin let out a held breath, her tail waving again as Omrak hacked and coughed. Daniel reached forwards and, gripping Omrak's upper body, ripped him from the opening. The large Northerner screamed as the ragged edges of the passageway tore his clothing and skin apart. Daniel unapologetically bent down, laying a Healer's Mark on the large Northerner before he turned back to scan for more trouble. The big Adventurer just curled up, hacking and coughing as he regained control of his body.

As Omrak slowly recovered, Daniel shifted his gaze to the Northerner every once in a while. That was too damn close.

Chapter 16

Hours of crawling, walking and climbing had left the group no closer to finding the exit. The ninth floor sprawled, with each cavern having multiple exits at any one time. Each of those exits, no matter how small, had to be verified and checked. And through all this, the party had to be wary of the slimes that could appear at any time, or the Crawlers that traversed the caverns.

One concern that Daniel held close to his chest was the potential that the Crawlers had blocked the staircase down, ensuring that the group would be unable to find the exit. It was a minor concern since they would eventually map the entire location and, if necessary, they could backtrack. The greater concern was that eventually the Elms would be here too, searching.

"Hold," Omrak said as he scrambled around in his pack to find another torch. Whenever they could, the group had used bigger passageways, if for no other reason than to not waste time as Omrak relit his torch. In the end, they had begun sending Asin ahead on smaller passageways to allow her to scout them out. It saved them time, especially as many of these passageways were found to be connected to another, previously explored location, or one that could be accessed more easily.

"Sure," Daniel said, settling in to watch for slimes. Asin ignored the command as she looked for additional passages. It was, after all, her role in the group.

"I disliked this section before," Omrak said, looking around the dimly lit location. The torch did little to increase the illumination in the caverns, instead layering slightly brighter spots over less illuminated areas. "It has not improved."

"These slimes are tough," Daniel said, shaking his head. "I regret giving up my bracers."

"Enchanted weaponry would be useful. My brother has an enchanted knife, one that burns with a flameless heat," Omrak said. "It would be useful here."

"Or a shovel," Daniel said. "Something to scoop the stones out."

"A shovel ..." Omrak rubbed his chin and then laughed. "That would work. Pity I did not bring one."

"Looks like she's ready." Daniel nodded up to Asin, who was waving them to her. "Time to get going."

"Yes." Omrak stepped forwards and then paused, clapping Daniel on the shoulder. "Thank you."

Daniel just nodded, embarrassed by the thanks. Chuckling, the Northerner walked forwards and ducked low as he got ready to squeeze into another too-tight passage.

***

Late that evening, the group had finally called it a day. They had covered a lot of ground but still had not found the exit. After careful scouting, Asin had determined that there were only a couple of entrances in the cavern they squatted in, giving them their best chance of a peaceful night's rest.

Not that they expected a good rest. It was clear that this floor was extremely busy with the slimes and Crawlers, ensuring that the group constantly had to be on watch. They would definitely have to rest in rotating watches.

"Should we go back?" Omrak asked, chewing on his dinner of dried beef jerky and bread.

"Why?" Asin asked.

"Both Daniel and I struggle with the slimes. It is only your Skills that have given us an edge. With appropriate equipment, we could travel faster," Omrak answered. Daniel stayed silent, content to let the two argue.

"How much? Map," Asin asked, turning to Daniel.

"Maybe half?" Daniel said. It was hard to tell, what with the sprawling passages that could cut off without warning.

"No," Asin said, shaking her head.

"Why?" Omrak growled. "Each fight is a risk for Daniel and me. It would be better for us to fight at full strength."

"One day. Half. Back. Half-day. No. Race," Asin explained, tail lashing out behind her angrily. After she was done, she rubbed at her throat. Talking so much always hurt.

Omrak just stared at Asin, confusion on his face, before looking to Daniel. He sighed and explained, "It's a half-day to get back. Then we're a half-day back in to where we are and maybe, we'd be faster. Probably. But it takes us only a day to finish half, so we only need a day to finish. That about right Asin?"

She nodded and then added one last word: "Race."

"Right, and we're in a race," Daniel said.

"You agree with her?" Omrak said, looking to the shorter Adventurer.

"I think … yes. I think we should push ahead. That was the plan," Daniel replied.

"Very well," Omrak conceded, looking somewhat annoyed but accepting. "I shall take first watch."

Daniel just nodded. He would take midwatch. His Gift let him last longer than the other two after all. Even a few hours' sleep would help them all, fitful and split as it might be.

***

Sleep that evening had been less than restful. The group had stumbled awake twice, fighting off the intrusion of a Crawler and then a group of slimes. Even then, the catnaps they had managed to catch had refreshed the group sufficiently enough that they were able to start exploring in the early hours of the morning. Now, in the midafternoon, the group were crouched, staring down at the enormous cavern laid out before them.

"What is that?" hissed Daniel as he stared at the green gelatinous cube that dominated the cavern before them. Unlike the other slimes, which were often only a foot or so across, this one was nearly six feet wide. It would be a simple matter for a creature that big to swallow an Adventurer whole.

"Big slime," Asin said, running a finger along a knife. Eyes narrowed, she searched for signs of the Mana Stone within its body. If they could destroy it, that would end the fight no matter how big the slime was.

"It must be the floor Champion," Omrak rumbled quietly.

"Definitely," Daniel confirmed, shaking his head as he considered his attack options. Shield Bash would do nothing to the monster, other than perhaps displacing some of its body. Neither Perin's Blow nor Double Strike would injure it, and his latest Skill Proficiency was not an active weapon. He could see where the Mana Stones were, but it did little good when the stones were embedded so deeply in the monster's body.

"I fear I would be of little use here," Omrak said, having done his own assessment as well. It would take a lot of torches to injure it and they just did not have the time.

"Around?" Asin pointed backwards and the group grimaced. One thing they had noticed with the new Dungeon layout was that often the staircase was situated very close to the Champions. It was a change from previous layouts and could potentially be just a matter of the lack of Adventurers sending the Champions to spawn again. In either case, the chances were that the staircase was near here—potentially just past the Floor Champion.

"Probably for the best," Daniel muttered at last. Omrak nodded and the group quietly creeped backwards. No sense in attempting a fight where two thirds of the group could do little to it. Still, Daniel pondered what they could do with what they had. Surely there was a way to win that fight.

***

Hours later, the group found themselves collected once more near the entrance to the Champion's chamber. Thus far, they had not seen sight nor sound of the Crimson Elms. Considering the size of the cavern, that meant very little. Still, the party held a little hope that they were still ahead of the Elms. Having explored the gaps in the maps in Daniel's mind, they now found themselves back where they started hours ago.

"Any ideas?" Daniel asked, staring at the chamber.

"I fight. Poison. Run," Asin said.

"That seems foolhardy," Omrak pointed out. "I would not agree to that."

"I have to agree. Your Skills might be the most effective, but it still takes a while for the slimes to die. Something that big …" Daniel said, shaking his head. "Going in alone is a bad idea."

Asin growled but just nodded, her tail lashing out behind her. She turned to stare at the pair, waiting to see if they had any other ideas.

"I was thinking …" Daniel started, and then stopped. A part of him seriously did not like the idea he was about to suggest. Old training, old habits, said it was a bad idea. Still, it was the only one that he could think of. At his friend's encouraging nods, he finally gives voice to his thoughts. "We could use oil. Douse it in the oil flasks we have left, set it on fire."

Omrak hummed, rubbing his chin in thought. "It is big enough. Though, such a large monster on fire …"

Daniel could see it in his mind's eye. A flaming cube that rolled around the cavern, setting everything it touched on fire. Worse, he knew that too much fire could potentially be dangerous for them—creating bad air that could hurt, maybe even kill the group. It was always a concern in real mines—though how it worked in a Dungeon, Daniel did not know. His little experience with the Dungeons indicated that they did not act the same way mines did, that concerns like bad air and buildup of dangerous gasses did not occur. Still…

"Idea?" Asin said, prodding Omrak, who shook his head. At that, Asin pointed to Daniel and finished the conversation. "Oil."

***

Saying it and doing it were two different things. The party quickly laid out their plans, divvying up the bottles and the last of the torches between

Daniel and Omrak. They would be in charge of throwing and lighting the monster on fire. Asin would creep into the room first and begin the attack, using her blades to damage and poison the monster immediately. Once the monster was focused on her, the pair would throw their oil flasks and hopefully set it on fire before retreating as Asin attacked it again.

At first, the entire plan went well. Asin's attacks left streaks of purple poison that slowly spread through the slime, injuring it. Interestingly enough, her knives never left the body of the creature, instead held and caught in the viscous liquid that was its body. The oil flasks, thrown at the monster, shattered, spreading its contents on the creature. Or in one case, was swallowed entirely. When the pair managed to stab the slime with their torches, it lit the flames and sent shudders through the Jell-O body.

What they did not expect was the way the monster then proceeded to swallow the majority of the flames into its body, extinguishing them within its core. So surprised were they that the pair nearly did not move away in time when the monster charged them, flames still licking along its surface. Scrambling backwards, the pair split up as they rounded a particularly wide stalagmite.

Behind, Asin hissed in anger as her poisoned and aura-enchanted blades continued to fly true and were ignored. She targeted all across the slime's body, determined to spread the poison faster as the monster kept its core away from her. Yet, nothing she did seemed to draw the monster's attention as it darted towards Daniel.

Daniel scurried away, trying to circle around the cavern, and give time for Asin and Omrak to continue their attacks. Omrak pulled his last flask from a pouch, throwing it at the monster. The oil relit on the dying flames on the surface of the slime's body, sending the slime shuddering as it started to twist its body inside out. Bereft of oil, Omrak pulled out his sword and targeted the edges of the creature, lopping off pieces. The shorter Adventurer darted in, using the edges of his shield to scoop out parts from the body as well. If they could not kill it with fire, they would have to do it the hard way.

Focused on attacking the monster, Daniel did not notice that the slime was no longer shuddering but rearing a portion of its body straight up. With a sploosh, the entire stretched cube fell on Daniel, engulfing him in the viscous fluid. Almost immediately, Daniel could feel the acidic properties of the slime start acting on his skin, attempting to eat away at his body.

Pain immediately filled his existence. The slime attacked his bare skin and slowly penetrated between his armor and clothing, burning layers of skin. Worse, it attacked his eyes, ears, and nose as it attempted to invade his body. Mouth closed, Daniel reached out to clamp a hand over his nose and squeeze it shut. As his body burned, Daniel attempted to focus to cast a spell, but pain robbed him of his concentration. Trapped in his body, Daniel could only squirm and thrash as the monster ate away at his body.

Omrak snarled in surprise, his sword flashing again and again as he carved bits of the monster. Asin dashed forwards as well, pulling her larger melee knives from her sheaths before she began slicing into the monster, dodging side to side after each strike. Each attack left streaks of purple in its body and sparks of electricity that fried and stilled the portions contacted. Yet, each of their attacks still did little to reduce the large slime that continued to strip the skin from Daniel's body.

Screaming in muted pain, his mouth clamped shut, Daniel reached inwards. He found his Gift, waiting as always for him. With a thought, Daniel released the Gift through his body and focused it on his senses, which were slowly being eaten away, patching his eyes and ears together even as he felt his memories disappear. His free hand continued to thrash about, trying to grip something, anything.

Seeing that his attacks were doing little, Omrak dodged to the side again and thrust his sword forwards. The blade plunged into the monster, piercing through gelatinous flesh all the way into Daniel's own body. In the beginning, the pain from being impaled was hidden beneath the cascade of other pain signals, but as Daniel's body thrashed around again, he finally noticed the shard of steel in his body. His free hand reached out and gripped the blade reflexively and then Omrak pulled the blade backwards. Daniel, his mind clouded, felt himself drawn forwards and gambled as he reached to grip the giant sword with both hands. Seeing that Daniel had a better grip now, Omrak tugged harder, drawing the Adventurer out of the body.

At first the slime did not notice their motions, focused as it was on the danger that Asin posed. However, as Daniel began to move through its body more quickly, the slime shifted, pulling its body to recover the beleaguered Adventurer. In doing so, the slime shifted its Mana core closer to the Catkin.

Asin snarled and lunged forwards, plunging her hand into the body up to her shoulder. The slime shuddered, its body trembling as the arcs of electricity that surrounded Asin's aura interacted with its body, injuring it. The slime stunned for a second, Asin was able to grasp the stone and yank backwards, extracting it finally from the slime.

Daniel, partially pulled outwards, fell to the ground as the monster exploded, its body no longer held together by the Mana Stone. Almost immediately, the slime's body began to disperse, leaving the stripped, partially digested body of the Adventurer on the floor. His Gift, running on automatic, patched his body together, replacing skin and muscle, repairing his eyes and ears. After a few minutes, Daniel was able to grasp hold of his senses and stop his Gift, using his Mana to cast a Healer's Mark on his own body.

Only when Daniel sat up did Asin come over, her own arm burnt and damaged from her attack. Daniel placed a healing on it too before he looked to Omrak, his eyes still blurry. For a moment, Daniel attempted to find the Northerner, and it was only Asin's guidance that he saw the blond Adventurer in the corner, throwing up.

Daniel tried to speak and coughed, his voice raw. He swallowed a few more times, casting a Minor Healing on himself before he could do so. "Is he okay?"

"Bad. No skin," Asin said, pointing to Daniel.

"Oh …" Daniel said. He began to think back to what had happened and flinched mentally as his mind refused to return to those dire minutes.

"Okay?" Asin asked softly, placing a hand on his shoulder.

"I … I will be," Daniel said finally as he sat up. As he raised a hand to brush his hair back, Daniel stared at the uncontrolled shaking in it. Perhaps he was more injured than he thought.

***

Finding the staircase down after Daniel had recovered only took them a few more hours. Before they had left, they had a spirited discussion on whether to go on. In the end, it was Daniel's insistence that they finish this—or at least, learn what the last floor was like—that drove them on. Injured, tired, and mentally scarred or not, they were nearly done.

As always, the annex for the tenth floor was a plain, bare room. The trio slowly stared around them, eyeing the simple wooden door that blocked the way in.

"Ready?" Daniel asked, a tightness in his chest as he stared at what might wait for them. This was it. One last floor, one last Boss. And then they would be done.

Asin just yowled while Omrak nodded. It was time to check out the last floor.

Chapter 17

The room that the three of them walked into was circular in design, reminiscent of an ancient colosseum. Clean brown sand, a wide-open sky and walls that were over ten feet high that led to a stand. The trio clumped together as they walked in, eyeing the empty stretch of sand.

"What is this?" Daniel muttered.

Asin shook her head, her tail lashing out behind her as she stalked forwards with an eye on the ground. The creaking of wooden winch made all three look up, staring as the gate ahead of them slowly opened. Out from the gate came a trundling boar that was over twenty feet tall, hairy bristles and long tusks snorting. Immediately on spotting the party, it rushed them, picking up speed as the three scattered, Asin to the far right and Omrak to Daniel's left.

"Why me?" Daniel cried out as he realized that the monster was charging him. It wasn't particularly surprising, since he was in the middle but Daniel could not help but feel somewhat prosecuted. Having realized he couldn't get away, Daniel hunkered down beneath his shield and reinforced the shield with his other hand, breathing slowly as he timed his counterattack.

With a roar, Daniel countercharged the monster and engaged his Shield Bash. The boar smashed him backwards, not even pausing as Daniel's attack connected and cracked his shield and a tusk at the same time. The Adventurer was thrown backwards, flying through the air to impact the wall and crash to the ground. The boar swerved away, ignoring the fallen Adventurer.

Omrak, having seen that he was not targeted, had charged back to the monster and, as it began its turn, swung his sword. Skin parted as the muscle was torn apart by the blade, ripping a deep gash on the boar's flank. As the boar finished its turn and charged towards Asin, Omrak dashed forwards to the slowly moving Daniel.

Asin snarled, running backwards as she threw another series of knives at the monster. Each of her attacks barely pricked the boar, its tough hide stronger than armor. Only a Piercing Shot had thus far managed to penetrate its body. Still, the Catkin did not give up as she sprinted to the wall as the monster bore down on her.

It was only a few seconds before it hit her that Asin jumped, claws extended as she sprawled against the wall and held on to it. The boar, unwilling to smash directly into the wall, was forced to swerve at the last second, only its tail brushing against Asin. Even that was enough to rip her away from the wall and leave a quickly blossoming bruise.

Spluttering, Daniel pushed himself upwards as Omrak put the waterskin away. Already the Northerner was moving away from Daniel, sword raised as the boar targeted him. He crouched low, sword held near his knee as he waited for the monster to arrive. Snorting and growling, the boar picked up speed as it closed in on Omrak.

Daniel pushed to his feet just as the boar collided with Omrak. Sword held low and pommel dug into the ground, the large Adventurer had used his large sword as an improvised spear and impaled the Boss monster on it. Thrown backwards from the impact, Omrak hit the wall and bounced off it before being trod upon by the boar's back foot.

Dashing over, Daniel placed a hand on Omrak's shoulder even as the big Adventurer struggled to his feet. Concentrating, Daniel laid

Healer's Mark on his friend and then Minor Healing, before he turned to search for the Boss. Asin, having run back, threw her bolas at the creature's leg in a vain attempt to trip the monster. The bolas caught but were so stretched out, they ripped apart without slowing the monster down. Thankfully, instead of directing itself at any single Adventurer, the board dashed to the other side of the arena as it built up speed again.

"You okay, Asin?" Daniel called out as she neared, placing Healer's Mark on her the moment she was within reach. It would help a little bit but for the most part, Daniel looked to conserve the remainder of his Mana for when it was going to be really needed.

Asin pulled another pair of throwing knives into her hand from her backpack, staring at the boar that had just turned around. Growling softly, the Catkin took off at an angled run, already throwing her knives at it, using Piercing Shot to help cover the distance.

"Crossbow," Omrak suggested as he stood up, searching for his sword. He spotted it a moment later, still embedded in the monster's body. The Northerner reached for his knife, taking off running, while Daniel sheathed his sword and reached for his slung crossbow.

A brief inspection showed that it was still working, if worse for wear. Quickly, Daniel cranked the crossbow back and pulled a bolt out before he tossed it away and reached for an unbroken one. The crossbow might have survived Daniel being thrown around, but it seemed that some of his bolts had not. Finally loaded, Daniel swung the crossbow back up to target the charging boar. At least, Daniel thought, even he could not miss a monster the size of a barn.

The boar had turned again and somehow, between the time that Daniel was loading his weapon and the last time he saw her, Asin had managed to mount the creature. Crouched above the monster, lightning arcs shooting as the monster contacted her body, the Catkin stabbed and cut with her weapons as she attempted to flay the monster alive.

Beneath her, the boar charged the Northerner, who stood, crouched and waiting. At the last moment, Omrak threw himself forwards, grabbing his sword and rolling to the side at the same time. The sword slid sideways as the opposing forces of the roll and charge tore open the wound, forcing a cascade of blood to pour out.

Daniel exhaled, firing his crossbow, and then reloaded immediately even as the creature turned, attempting to come around and attack the beleaguered, blond Adventurer. Omrak, clipped by a hoof, struggled to his feet, his sword behind him as the boar finally slowed down and turned to attack, only to receive another crossbow bolt in its face. It snorted and squealed but stayed on task as it moved to gore Omrak.

Omrak in turn swung and cut at the creature's nose, forcing the monster to be wary of his attacks. No longer charging, the monster did not have the impetus of its momentum to bowl over the large Northerner and so they feinted with sword and tusk. All the while, Daniel and Asin continued to attack it.

"It's slowing down!" Daniel said as he dropped in another bolt. The successive attacks and blood loss was taking its toll along with the continued presence of the enchanted Catkin above and her poisoned weapons. Strong and powerful as the boar was, it could only take so much damage.

Ducking a swipe with one tusk, Omrak stood and lunged forwards, blade sinking into a cheek before he attempted to tear the blade free. However, unbeknownst to Omrak, his sword was stuck between some teeth which caused his motion to grind to a stop. In that brief moment, the boar twisted its head again to lash out with its remaining tusk. Omrak was thrown to the side, his back torn wide open.

Daniel shouted out loud in the vain hope of attracting the monster's attention as he ran forwards, holding the crossbow up to his body as he closed the distance to his fallen friend. Closer now, he raised the weapon and, working on intuition, pulled the trigger and sent the bolt flying to embed in the boar's eye. The monster snorted and jerked reflexively as it was blinded, having missed Omrak's prone form by inches as it slammed into the wall.

Asin was thrown to the side by the impact, unseated from the top of the monster but the Catkin hung on grimly as she plunged her knife once again into the monster's body. Even now, she could see the slow spreading of the poison. All they needed to do was wait and her Skill would kill it.

Bent over Omrak, Daniel swiftly cast his Minor Healing spell once and then again before he surged to his feet. Hefting his remaining weapon, Daniel got ready to do battle with the Boss. Crouched low, he grimaced as a sharp pain in his lower back shot up his spine. He shook his head, focusing on the monster, and decided to try Perin's Blow as the monster lunged forwards. Tusk smashed backwards, the boar growled and flicked its head, its mane flowing out behind it. While the monster was dazed, Daniel lashed out with his mace, beating on the monster's snout and pulping it, sending the monster into a rage.

As Daniel attracted the monster's attention in front, Omrak staggered to the side, his body leaking red light. He roared as he reared back, sword held in hand, then he swung downwards, shearing through the boar's front right leg. As the boar collapsed, Asin threw herself off, rolling and rolling before struggling to her feet and spitting to clear her mouth of sand.

The trio quickly backed off from the crippled Boss. Daniel sagged to the ground as the injuries to his body finally caught up to him. Beside him, Omrak roared as the red light continued to glow from his body, while Asin hastened the monster's death by tossing the last few of her knives.

Enraged and stubborn, the boar pulled itself along the ground, inching towards Omrak, who stood, waiting. When it was finally in range, the large Northerner stabbed his sword into its eye, driving the blade all the way into the brain. A last, shuddering jerk sent Omrak flying one last time before the monster died.

"Daniel?" Asin said, walking over to her friend. The short Adventurer waved her away, slanted eyes tightening in pain as he waited for the Healer's Mark he had placed on himself to do its job. It would not heal him fully, but it was all that he could do.

Omrak, curled up on his side, was unconscious when Asin managed to make her way to him. She prodded him a few times before she gave up, sitting down to watch over her friends as they recovered.

Chapter 18

A half-hour later, Daniel finally sat back up and walked over to Asin. Omrak continued to snore, his body drained from the fights. Daniel frowned, touching him for a brief moment to ascertain that he would survive, before he walked over to the large chest that Asin has been staring at.

"That our winnings?" Daniel asked, pointing.

Asin nodded, fished in her pockets, and pulled out the largest and clearest Mana Stone Daniel had ever seen.

"What is that? A B class four?" Daniel said.

Asin, for once, just shrugged. It was not as if she had seen a stone like this before. It was certainly an improvement over the B Class 12 that the previous Karlak Boss had given out.

"Did you open it??" Daniel asked, pointing to the chest, and Asin shook her head. She sighed, going back to staring at the chest. After a moment, Daniel walked over to Omrak and prodded him with his foot in an attempt to wake him. It took the careful use of his Gift to prod the Northerner awake.

Omrak rose from the ground, sword clutched in his hand, to stare at the empty field of battle.

He groaned slightly, head still hurting from repeated hits, before he spotted the chest and relaxed.

The group, gathered together, stood and stared at the chest, wondering what was within.

"Asin?" Daniel finally said, pushing the patiently waiting Catkin.

No sooner had the words left his mouth than was the Catkin pounced forwards, pulling the chest open. Within, there were two pieces of equipment. A simple hammer with an engraving on it, and a thin, black leather breastplate. The three Adventurers looked at the equipment, frowning, before the Catkin picked them up and handed them around.

Daniel clutched the hammer, staring at the spike that protruded from one end, and looked at the group, who just gave him a slight nod. Omrak took the breastplate, his hands running over the leather.

"This is magical," Omrak said.

"Should be," Daniel answered, sliding the hammer into his pack. It was obvious that the hammer with its etched runes was definitely enchanted in some form. Better not to use it yet.

"We can ask around to get them identified. When we're back."

"Asin, you are bereft of a prize," Omrak said.

"Stone. Mine," Asin said, patting her hip.

Daniel just nodded happily in agreement while Omrak glanced at Asin's pouch and then the armor in his hand. Finally, he nodded. Daniel understood what he probably was thinking, that they had no way to tell how powerful or even if the item itself was not cursed. But that was part of the gamble of being an Adventurer.

***

The three Adventurers slowly limped out of the Dungeon, their movements slowed down from exhaustion and injuries. Yet all three could not help but trade grins with one another and the guards as they exited.

"Did you finish it?" Ken asked, the large guard holding back a smile.

"Yes," Daniel said, and Ken raised a hand to clap his friend on the back and then decided against it. Daniel was not healed enough for that kind of boisterous congratulations.

"Tough fight?" Ken's question was more a statement. Daniel offered a slight nod before he gestured to his friends who had not stopped walking. "Go."

Daniel quickly hurried to catch up with his friends as they entered the Adventurers' Guild, managing to do so before they entered the hall. As they walked in, the Guild slowly fell silent as Adventurers and attendants spotted the trio. An Adventurer who was working with Liev quickly stepped aside as he waved the three of them forwards. Something showed on his face, something that Daniel could not place, but which twisted his stomach.

"Liev," Daniel said as he pulled the hammer from his belt. Asin had already reached for her pouches, placing the pair down and pulling down the edges of one to reveal the Boss Mana Stone. Omrak was slower as he struggled to pull the leather armor from his pack, but he eventually did. Through all this, the silence resounded through the room, stretching tight.

"Daniel. Asin. Omrak," Liev said calmly. He reached out and touched the Boss Mana Stone and slowly turned it about. When he next spoke, the redhead tried to keep his voice professional. "Congratulations."

"Did we do it?" Daniel said, somehow knowing the answer.

"No," Liev replied, shaking his head. "The Elms were in half a day ago. I'm sorry."

The three groaned in unison, their faces fallen as they traded looks between one another. Half a day. They were short by just a little. If they had explored a little more the day before, if they had skipped sleeping. If they had the right weapons. Around them, now that the bad news had been imparted, the Guild came back to life.

"You'll want to speak with Tharuk about the hammer," Liev continued, fingers lightly brushing the steel weapon. "I'm sure he'll be able to verify its details. As for this." Liev reached out to run a finger along the edges of the armor. "May I?"

After Omrak's agreement, Liev hefted the armor, running his fingers along the seams and down the bare front of the armor. He turned it inside out, staring at the clear back before he brushed a sharp fingernail along the front once more. Finally, he placed it back down on the counter. "This is unenchanted, as you probably guessed. No runes, no markings. Remarkably resilient, though. I would say it's from a Black Rhinoceros."

"Unenchanted?" Omrak repeated, his face crestfallen.

"Yes. It's very difficult to enchant Black Rhinoceros hide. Even untreated, it's stronger than most iron," Liev said. "Save enough, get a good Enchanter, and you'd have an amazing piece of armor."

Omrak's face lit up again as he took back the armor, stuffing the supple but tough piece into his pack. Asin, who had been quietly watching, prodded the stone, her ears tilted down. Liev smiled slightly, pulling the stone closer for inspection.

Daniel turned away while Liev spoke with Asin, rubbing at his eyes where tears threatened to spill. Damn it. They had been so close. Exhaustion combined with the comedown from the fights and delve threatened to break his control. He could not help but think that this was expected.. They were an Advanced Team after all. They never stood a chance.

"Daniel?" Liev called again, and the short Adventurer blinked, turning back to the counter.

On the counter was a crystal ball, one that he had not seen in ages. "If you'll extend your hand?"

Daniel slowly complied and, guided by Liev, placed his hand on the crystal ball. It flared to life for a moment, Liev murmuring arcane words as he adjusted Daniel's status.

"Done."

Daniel smiled slightly, pulling his hand back from the crystal. Like his friends, he decided to take a look at his newly updated Status.

Name: Daniel Chai (Advanced Rank Adventurer)

Class: Level 9 Adventurer (63%)

Sub-classes: Level 7 (Miner) (04%)

Human (Male)

Statistics

Life: 281

Stamina: 281

Mana: 206

Attributes

Strength: 27

Agility: 24

Constitution: 30

Intelligence: 21

Willpower: 20

Luck: 15

Skills

Unarmed Combat: Level 3 (93/100)

Clubs (Novice): Level 2 (17/100)

Archery: Level 2 (68/100)

Shield (Novice): Level 1 (24/100)

Dodge: Level 7 (83/100)

Combat Sense: Level 7 (78/100)

Perception: Level 7 (56/100)

Mining: Level 7 (78/100)

Healing (Novice): Level 1 (41/100)

Herb Lore: Level 3 (31/100)

Stealth: Level 2 (24/100)

Cooking: Level 4 (03/100)

Singing: Level 2 (14/100)

Skill Proficiencies

Double Strike

Shield Bash

Perin's Blow

Find Weakness

Mapping (II)

Spells

Minor Healing (II)

Healer's Mark (I)

Gifts

Martyr's Touch—The caster may heal oneself or others by touch and concentration, sacrificing a portion of his life to do so. Cost varies depending on the extent of the injuries healed.

Later that day, the three Adventurers found themselves seated in the Spinning Top, nursing their injuries and sorrows. Their initial elation over completing the Dungeon had disappeared long ago and now the three sat, nursing their food in silence. They had failed at the quest, failed to beat the Elms.

Khy'ra walked into the inn and leaned against the doorway for a second, staring at her boyfriend before she sighed, noting how the glum trio had infected the entire Inn with their sorrow. Taking a seat next to her boyfriend, the Elf tilted her head as Daniel looked up at her.

"Is this how a team that just completed their first Dungeon looks like now?" Khy'ra asked, shaking her head. "I might be old, but surely the time traditions haven't changed that much."

"We lost," Daniel said, running a finger around some spilled beer. "By half a day."

"And?" Khy'ra said, shaking her head. "Did it mean you didn't get your Dungeon completion equipment? Did you miss out on the Stone itself?"

"No …" Daniel said, noting the tone she held. He knew what was coming.

"Then celebrate," Khy'ra said, rapping her knuckles on the table to get the attention of the other two. Not that they were not listening in already. "Last lesson. There's always something wrong, always something depressing about this job. A bad delve, a lost friend, a missed quest. This job, this career, it's all about regrets. Always, always celebrate your successes. Otherwise, put your hammer down now. If you cannot celebrate when it is called for, you are in the wrong profession. It only gets harder from now on."

Daniel cast his head down, his hand caressing the hammer he had just won. He looked at Khy'ra and she flashed him a smile, and he found himself reaching for her hand, squeezing it. This success, this win, was a bittersweet one for her too. And yet, she was smiling.

Celebrate when you can …

"Elise! A round for everyone," Daniel said, calling to the innkeeper and forcing a smile on his face. Omrak roared his approval, pounding his drink on the table and splashing Asin who growled at the large, loud Adventurer.

"Noisy!"

***

A week later, the trio found themselves meeting up in the Top in the early morning. Daniel rushed down the stairs, shirt still untucked as he hauled his packed bag with him. Below, Asin and Omrak rolled their eyes as the Adventurer arrived late once again.

"Sorry, sorry!" Daniel apologized as he sighted his friends.

"Khy'ra?" Asin asked, looking up the staircase.

"Coming," Khy'ra said, following behind Daniel at a more sedate pace and giving the Catkin a quick hug. "I wouldn't miss seeing you off."

"School?" Asin said once she was released.

"Don't worry. The Stone will keep them fed for a while and we wrangled a slight return of the funds. Being a local hero gave your dad some leverage with the Council," Khy'ra assured the Beastkin. "And I promise, your dad and I will make sure the funds you send back get put to good use."

"Goodbye," Asin said, her face falling slightly before she stepped away.

"This is for lunch," Elise said, walking out with a series of wrapped packages that she quickly distributed. "Don't forget, Mary's still waiting for you. And I'll expect a letter once in a while."

Daniel nodded, hand gripping Khy'ra's. The Catkin and Northerner shared a look before they walked out, leaving the two lovebirds alone.

"Khy'ra …" Daniel started, before he was hushed by a finger on his lips.

"No. We said it all. Did it all," Khy'ra said, eyes twinkling slightly at the last. "It's enough. You have a life to live. And so do I. Come back, when you can. Write, when you can. But live your life."

Daniel smiled slightly, kissing her fingers, and nodded. He turned, walking away, and rubbed at his eyes as he left to join the pair who dutifully ignored him as they left the city. On the road, outside, the trio looked at one another.

"Is this the right road to Peel?" Daniel finally said as they trudged along.

"No," Asin stated, glaring at him.

Daniel blinked, mouthed *oops* as they turned around. The trio laughed, shaking their heads as they made their way to the next Dungeon.

Author's Note

If you enjoyed reading the book, please do leave a review and rating. Not only is it a big ego boost, it also helps sales and convinces me to write more in the series!

If you enjoyed this, check out my other series:
- Life in the North (An Apocalyptic LitRPG)

https://readerlinks.com/l/729295
- A Gamer's Wish (An Urban Fantasy LitRPG)

https://readerlinks.com/l/729151
- A Thousand Li (a cultivation series inspired by Chinese wuxia and xianxia novels)

https://readerlinks.com/l/729231

For more great information about LitRPG series, check out the Facebook groups:
- Gamelit Society

https://www.facebook.com/groups/LitRPGsociety/
- LitRPG Books

https://www.facebook.com/groups/LitRPG.books/

About the Author

Tao Wong is an avid fantasy and sci-fi reader who spends his time working and writing in the North of Canada. He's spent way too many years doing martial arts of many forms and having broken himself too often, now spends his time writing about fantasy worlds.

If you'd like to support him directly, Tao now has a Patreon page where previews of all his new books can be found!
https://www.patreon.com/taowong

For updates on the series and the author's other books (and special one-shot stories), please visit his website: http://www.mylifemytao.com

Subscribers to Tao's mailing list will receive exclusive access to short stories in the Thousand Li and System Apocalypse universes:
https://www.subscribepage.com/taowong

Or visit his Facebook Page:
https://www.facebook.com/taowongauthor

About the Publisher

Starlit Publishing is wholly owned and operated by Tao Wong. It is a science fiction and fantasy publisher focused on the LitRPG & cultivation genres. Their focus is on promoting new, upcoming authors in the genre whose writing challenges the existing stereotypes while giving a rip-roaring good read.

For more information on Starlit Publishing, visit our website!
https://www.starlitpublishing.com/

You can also join Starlit Publishing's mailing list to learn of new, exciting authors and book releases.
https://starlitpublishing.com/newsletter-signup/

Read an excerpt of Book 4 of Adventures on Brad series:
The Arena's Call

Chapter 1

Separated from the trio of heroes by a simple metal gate, the twelve-foot-long, luminescent green scaled and squat drake lay dozing in the Mana-lit cavern. Enclosed all around by cold stone, the drake slumbered fitfully, the silence only broken by the slow drip of water that formed a pool in the corner. As the trio watched, the drake yawned lazily and showed the inside of its pink mouth, one filled with rows upon rows of sharp, deadly teeth.

"I am not enjoying these surprises," Omrak said softly while the trio edged backwards from the metal gate. Reaching over his broad shoulders, the giant blond Northerner pulled his large two-handed sword from its utilitarian sheath to eye the blade.

"Well, it's just a single Dungeon Champion," Daniel Chai said as he adjusted his shield. His plate mail armor clanking slightly as he moved, the shorter, slant-eyed and flat-nosed Adventurer added, "I rather like the change after fighting all those lizards."

"Tough," Asin hissed, her furry tail lashing out beside her as cat ears twitched, clawed hands kneading the soil as she watched behind them. Her short cloak covered her body, helping her to hide in the shadows she'd instinctively found, her dark fur blending in.

"I agree with Hero Asin," Omrak growled. "A drake is significantly tougher than what we have dealt with before."

"Too tough for us?" Daniel asked, eyes narrowing even further to slits. While no longer a Beginner Adventurer, Daniel knew he was still new to the adventuring lifestyle. It had not even been two years since he left his lifestyle as a Miner.

"For us heroes? Nay. We should be able to defeat this opponent," Omrak said with renewed confidence. The teenager flashed a grin, lazily swinging the sword around his hand as he limbered up. "I but spoke for caution, to temper overconfidence. A hero must understand themselves."

Asin chuffed slightly, her back arching and tail straightening for a second as her cat ears tilted downward. Daniel coughed at the same time as he stopped the bubbling laughter. Omrak telling them to not be overconfident. Daniel found himself smiling, the spike of concern fading.

"Start," Asin said and walked over to the wooden lever that controlled the gate. She regarded her friends one last time to receive their agreement before she pulled on the device. Daniel shifted forward, his heavy crossbow in hand, a bulbous bolt locked in place.

With a screech, the pulley rose to the clanking of chains. As the noise reverberated around the cavern, the drake woke from its sleep. Twisting its long, sinuous neck towards the source of the noise, it hissed at Omrak who was in the process of ducking underneath the rising blockade.

"Come. Let us do battle and determine our worthiness!" Omrak roared his challenge and kept the monster's attention as he strode in, his simple, black leather breastplate made of monster hide the Northerner's only protection. In retaliation, the drake roared back its challenge.

"Good," whispered Daniel, the crossbow snug against his shoulder as he crouched. He gently squeezed the trigger, the crossbow kicking back as he targeted the monster's open mouth. Not realising he was doing it, Daniel held his breath as the bolt spun through the air and missed the open mouth, slamming into the creature's neck. A small explosion resulted as the explosive bolt triggered, tearing off scales and making the monster scream again.

"Missed!" Asin laughed, lobbing a knife underhand. The knife glowed as it flew through the air as Asin activated **Piercing Shot**, allowing the throwing knife to drill into the drake's mouth. The monster roared, the pain making the creature thrash. Its long tail swung around, careening like the end of a catapult into Omrak who had charged forwards to close the distance.

Omrak snarled as he blocked the attack, sword held at an angle as the tail impacted against the weapon and his body. The giant Northerner's feet skidded backwards, digging into the ground and throwing up soil before the monster's momentum finally came to an end. Omrak's sword glowed slightly under his Skill, the drake's tail notched from the blocked blow, scales crushed and blood beginning to fall. Taking advantage of the momentarily slowed appendage, Asin bounded up the creature's body before flinging herself high into the air. Knives held beneath her, she landed with a thump on the monster's back. Rearing itself backward in pain, the drake roared once more in an attempt to throw the Catkin off, even as she wrapped her feet around its body.

"What was that?" Daniel shouted as he rushed forwards, his crossbow discarded as he drew his enchanted hammer and shield. As the drake swung its head towards Daniel, he skidded and fought for purchase on loose sand and slick stone.

Asin ignored her partner's incredulous shout, too busy attempting to lever a scale off the monster's back. Even as she did so, arcs of electricity danced from her body into the drake's, the enchanted bracers she wore continually pulling electricity from the environment and her aura and grounding it in her foe's body.

Omrak snarled, swinging his great sword with both hands as he struck the drake. Anger coursing through his body at being ignored for his friends, the Northerner swung, again and again, trading ferocity for skill. Even as he righted himself from a stumble, he overextended and was forced to throw himself down to escape a grasping claw.

Struggling to his feet and running forwards, Daniel focused and triggered his skill **Shield Bash.** The attack slammed the monster's lunging jaws into the air as he pushed forth with his feet. With quick steps, Daniel swung the spike on his hammer into the exposed wound in the drake's neck as the head retracted from the initial attack. The spike sunk nearly all the way to the hilt before being ripped out, followed shortly by a flood of blood.

The drake hissed in pain and swung its head at Daniel. This time, Daniel was unable to block it in time, the blow sending him skidding across the ground before ending at the wall. Lying on the ground, Daniel groaned, grateful that the plate armour he wore absorbed the majority of the impact. He focused for a second, casting a **Healer's Mark** on his body, starting the healing process to deal with the incipient bruises and pulled muscles.

"Nay, your battle is with me!" roared Omrak as the drake attempted to rush Daniel. His shout triggered his ability **Challenge of the North**, drawing the drake's unwilling form to attack him again. Head lowered, it swiped with its front claw only to be blocked by Omrak's great sword.

Grinning, Daniel stood up and adjusted his helmet before he took off running, listening to Omrak's continued taunts and Asin's yowling as her enchantments took their toll on the monster's body. *Time to finish this*, Daniel thought.

***

As the drake let loose one last roar and collapsed almost on Omrak, Daniel exhaled with relief. As Asin tried to sit up from the floor, Daniel pushed her back down with one hand.

"Lie down damnit!" Daniel growled. "I've got to set your hip first unless you want it to heal crooked."

"Hurts!" Asin yowled but complied, her claws kneading the loose sand as she focused on the large Dungeon Champion's corpse. The Champion glowed for a moment, its body breaking apart as the Mana that held it together dispersed. With a light tinkle, the blue-grey Mana stone dropped to the ground, almost making Asin sit up again. Only a flash of pain as Daniel set her hip stopped her.

"Ah, here's the chest!" Omrak happily tromped over to the chest and on Asin's gold-filled heart. With a careless heave, Omrak opened the chest, curiosity driving his actions. Too late, Daniel noticed the Northerner's carelessness as the chest released a cloud of gas into Omrak's face. Coughing and wiping at his face, Omrak staggered back.

"Idiot. You're supposed to check first!" Daniel snarled as he finished casting **Minor Healing (II)** on Asin before he strode over to Omrak. "Hold still." With deft movements, Daniel gripped the Northerner by his leather tunic and splashed water over the man's face.

"Hero Daniel. I cannot see." Omrak said, his voice higher than normal, almost panicked.

"It's fine. Just hold still," Daniel said soothingly. One hand shifted to grip the blond giant's arm, the skin contact required for Daniel to trigger his Gift. That was what society called it – a Gift – but for those individuals like Daniel, born with an unexplained power, it was often a burden - for every Gift had a price.

As Daniel extended his Gift into Omrak's body, a flood of information flowed into his mind. The slightly pulled hamstring. The twisted ankle. The bunion that was growing on Omrak's foot. The poison that had invaded Omrak's eyes, blocking the nerves that gave sight. All this and more swept into Daniel's consciousness. It only took a gentle nudge, the slightest exertion of power to begin the cleansing process. And all it cost Daniel was a memory, a moment of his life. Daniel once again felt it slip from his mind, like an eel from a child's hand.

"Now, come here," Daniel guided Omrak to the wall and sat the man down gently. "Your sight will return in a little while. Till then, sit and think about what you did, you big lunk."

"My apologies, Hero Daniel," Omrak rumbled, bobbing his head in shame.

"No traps," Asin announced behind the pair triumphantly, having taken the time to review the once trapped chest. The Catkin then reached inside and fished out a single item - a curved knife in a sheath. On closer inspection, the group noticed runes that indicated that the weapon was likely enchanted.

"Only one?" Daniel said, disappointment tingeing his voice. After all, Karlak had given them two items in the final chest.

"One." Asin nodded, ears pointed downwards slightly, her tail drooping.

"What! Is there only one treasure?" Omrak shouted as he pushed himself to his feet, hands waving around in front of him.

"Sit down," Daniel snapped at Omrak. "And yes, there's only one."

"Do you think the trap destroyed the other?" Omrak asked guiltily.

"No," Asin said snippily before she walked over to the Northerner and lifted the Mana stone from his pouch.

"What…? Is that you, Asin?" Omrak said, patting at his newly emptied pouch. "Wait! You only took the stone, right? Asin?"

"She's gone," Daniel sighed, shaking his head. Thankfully the Peel Dungeon had an exit from the Dungeon Champion's cavern. It saved the team from having to trek through the previous floors on their way out of the Dungeon after completing it.

"Why did she leave?" Omrak said, frowning as he turned to where Daniel sat. "Did I do something wrong?"

"No. We're just on a timetable. The Guild closes earlier in Peel, remember?" Daniel patiently explained. With nothing better to do, Daniel pulled his hammer out and began the laborious process of cleaning his weapon. As the silence lengthened, broken only by the swish of cloth on metal, Omrak cleared his throat.

"Yes?" Daniel said.

"Can you tell me a story?" Omrak said, flushing slightly.

"A story?" Daniel said.

"Or just speak," Omrak said hurriedly. "It's just, sitting in the dark in the Dungeon…"

"Sorry," Daniel said with shame. Of course, Omrak was feeling somewhat uncertain. They had spent the last five days battling their way down the Peel Dungeon's floors, fighting smart lizard creatures who set traps, ran away and otherwise harried the team. As their vanguard, Omrak had suffered the most from the constant sniping attacks.

"My grandfather once told me this story, about the god Hanna. You know of her?" At

Omrak's nod, Daniel continued. "This was long ago. Long before Ba'al broke into Brad, when there were no Dungeons, and the Immortal War had not been fought. It was a more peaceful time when Erlis's children were numerous and lived with her in her silver palace. Now, Hanna was, and still is, mischievous. Rather than stay at home, she would often sneak down to our plane to frolic with the animals.

"On this day, she found a horse whose coat was the purest white but for the blood that marred it and the wounds that the blood originated from. Hanna rushed forwards, grasping the horse by the side and asked it what had happened. A single touch on the wounds and Hanna pulled her hand back, for the wounds were poisoned. Poisoned with a substance that Hanna had never seen before. But Hanna was a god, a minor god perhaps, but a god and so she vowed to cure the horse."

Caught in the story, Daniel forgot to wipe down his hammer. Instead, he was taken back, to a simpler time when it was just him and his grandfather. A time where the ring of pickaxes would resound from the mines, the never-ending creak of wheels as they rolled new ore out. A more peaceful time.

"Hanna brought back herbs that could cure any poison upon touch. Flowers that when crushed and mixed cleansed the body. Spells, chanted under breath, to drive toxins out. But nothing worked, no herb, no flower, no spell worked. In desperation, she searched through the mud and pulled out leeches, setting them upon the wound. These leeches would suck, drink the foul poison of the wounds and fall aside, twitching. And still, the wound festered, the horse slowly dying."

"Surely it did not die?" Omrak said, head tilted to his friend. This was a story he had not heard.

"Patience, friend. The story is not over. When all hope seemed lost, when the beast lay on the ground, Hanna struck upon one last, desperate idea. Holding forth her own arm, she sliced it open with her knife. Her blood fell, mixing with the toxin. Finally, finally, the toxins left the beast, pushed away by Hanna's divine blood. And so, the horse was healed. But another miracle occurred that day. For divine blood mixed with mortal and through Hanna's sacrifice, the horse transformed. For now, on its head, a single horn grew, a facet of the divine."

"A unicorn!" Omrak cried. "Divine creatures, sacred to all."

"Yes, a unicorn," Daniel said with a smile.

"That was a good story," Omrak said with a smile. "And I think I can see again. At least, enough for us to exit."

"Good. I'm glad you liked it," Daniel said with a smile as he walked over to help his friend stand. Together, the pair exited the Dungeon slowly. Yet, Daniel could not help but remember the last part of the story, the part that Omrak had interrupted him from telling. For the toxins, driven away by the divine blood, would pool with the leeches that fell earlier. And together, they would mutate, creating the first demon-born. Creatures that held a Mana stone – the blood of the divine – in their body which gave them form.

***

Later that evening, when things had quietened down, Daniel finally had time to check his notification. Lying in bed, he had to smile. Finally! He had finally achieved his tenth Level and gained access to the Adventurer's Special Skill – Inventory. It had only taken grinding through the entirety of the Peel Dungeon, killing the Dungeon Champion and getting the Dungeon completion reward. Admittedly, he perhaps shouldn't have used his Gift on that child…

With a quick wave of his hand, Daniel allocated his free attribute points and pushed away his thoughts. Done was done. Two to intelligence, one each to the physical attributes. He was still a front-line fighter after all and while Willpower allowed him to push through the pain and fear that could afflict him, what the team needed more was regular healing. It was, partially, what kept them in the game.

Content with his decision, Daniel flicked his hand and pulled up his character screen to review it in detail.

Name: Daniel Chai (Advanced Rank Adventurer)

 Class: Level 10 Adventurer (33%)

 Sub-classes: Level 7 (Miner) (04%)

 Human (Male)

Statistics

Life: 296

Stamina: 296

Mana: 217

Attributes

Strength: 28

Agility: 25

Constitution: 31

Intelligence: 23

Willpower: 20

Luck: 15

Skills

Unarmed Combat: Level 3 (93/100)

Clubs (Novice): Level 4 (37/100)

Archery: Level 2 (88/100)

Shield (Novice): Level 2 (64/100)

Dodge: Level 9 (03/100)

Combat Sense: Level 9 (18/100)

Perception (Novice): Level 1 (06/100)

Mining: Level 7 (78/100)

Healing (Novice): Level 2 (48/100)

Herb Lore: Level 3 (42/100)

Stealth: Level 2 (29/100)

Cooking: Level 4 (13/100)

Singing: Level 2 (14/100)

Skill Proficiencies

Double Strike

Shield Bash

Perin's Blow

Find Weakness

Mapping (II)

Inventory (Adventurer Special)

Spells

Minor Healing (II)

Healer's Mark (I)

Gifts

Martyr's Touch—The caster may heal oneself or others by touch and concentration, sacrificing a portion of his life to do so. Cost varies depending on the extent of the injuries healed.

Continue reading here:
https://readerlinks.com/l/729279

www.ingramcontent.com/pod-product-compliance
Lightning Source LLC
Chambersburg PA
CBHW060909210726
48293CB00006B/2023